MW00526319

# Storm

## *Jay Lang*

Print ISBNs
Amazon Print 978-0-2286-1653-5
LSI Print 978-0-2286-1654-2
BWL Print 978-0-2286-1655-9

*BWL Publishing Inc.*

*Books we love to write ...*
*Authors around the world.*

http://bwlpublishing.ca

# Chapter One

*My decision to get out of bed would have differed greatly if I had known what was to come—a confrontation with two killers who were preying on the most beautiful girl I had ever seen.*

\* \* \*

The faint scratching noise on the window over my bed instantly reminds me that I forgot to feed the neighborhood feral cat. If I ignore him, he'll start wailing until my neighbors shout profanities.

After quickly searching through the cupboards and coming up empty, the old Tom starts to yowl. Dammit! With no choice, I slide on my runners, grab my wallet and keys then head to the car—a 20-year-old Ford shit-box that a former co-worker gifted me.

As soon as I pull out of the underground lot, sheets of rain hammer down on the windshield. I glance at the time on the dash. 10:45 PM. With fifteen minutes until the store closes, I drive as fast as I dare on the dark backroad and arrive with a few moments to spare. I park amongst a group of cars that are huddled together not far from the entrance, then run to the door, a hand over my head in a vain attempt to stay dry.

Basket in hand, I walk fast-paced to the pet food lane. Just as I'm finished grabbing the small tins of cat grub and chucking them in my basket, a girl I don't recognize appears at the end of the aisle.

She has long dark hair and a thick, muscular build. The shininess of her short leather jacket and the dark spots on her jeans tells me she's been out in the rain for a while. She's too far away to make out her features but from her body language, she looks fidgety and doesn't seem to be shopping. I don't have time to study her—the store's closing. I turn my back to her and make my way to the till. As I stand in line behind a couple of shoppers, I keep an eye out for the mysterious woman.

After I've paid for the cat food, I exit the store, the night manager locking the door behind me. The rain has let up a little but not much. I quickly make my way over to my car and stand there, fumbling for my keys, and getting drenched. Just as I locate my keys in my pants pocket, I hear the scuffle of feet and look up. It's her, the dark-haired girl from the store.

With the light from the neon sign shining on us, I see her face clearly—exotic and stunningly beautiful. Her hair is wet and clinging to her olive skin while remnants of mascara sit just above her defined cheekbones. She nervously bites her full bottom lip. We stand staring at each other until the rev of an approaching vehicle breaks our concentration. She glances over her shoulder at the noise, then quickly crouches down between my vehicle and the one next to me.

The noisy car comes into view and drives in front of me. It's a newer model blue sedan. I get a quick look at the driver and passenger—two men about forty with short, dark hair. The eyes of the driver pierce through me as the car slowly passes by.

They drive slowly around the other parked cars. It's obvious they're looking for someone. I glance down at the beautiful stranger who is now crouched in a river of cold water.

"They're after you, aren't they?"

She nods. "Do you think you could give me a ride out of here?" Her dark eyes look terrified and desperate.

The logical part of my brain tells me to get in my car, lock my doors and call the cops, but a burning deep in my gut wants to help her. I quickly open the driver's door and flick the unlock button before climbing in and starting the engine.

I look in the rear-view mirror and watch as the back door opens and the girl slinks onto the backseat, closing the door softly.

I am just about to put the car into reverse when the blue car squeals up and stops in front of me. Instantly, I feel the air leave my lungs.

My heart racing, I clutch the wheel and stare between the moving wipers. I watch as the passenger door opens, and a thinly built man gets out. He walks up to my door. I slowly unwind my window.

"Hello. I am looking for my sister." The man has an Eastern European accent. "She has long dark hair and is wearing a black leather jacket. She's very sick and she needs help. Have you seen her?"

Before I can answer, his attention shifts to the back of my car. Thankfully, rain is blanketing the windows, making it difficult to see anything in the dark rear seats. As long as she doesn't move...

"No, I haven't," I say loudly, taking his attention from the backseat.

He stares at me for a few moments before turning and walking back to the blue car. I let out a long breath.

It's obvious that the woman isn't related to him. They look completely different and based on the thug's accent, they aren't even the same nationality. I slowly put the car in reverse and back up. The blue car inches forward toward me. Just as I turn the wheel and put the car into drive, they pull up alongside me. The driver's window goes down and the two men glare at me.

"Are you sure you haven't seen her?" the driver asks with the same accent as his passenger.

"I'm positive," I say, trying to keep eye contact.

Then, I catch a glimpse of something shiny in the hand of the other man. It only takes a second to identify the object as a knife, a long one with serrated edges. He's pretending to clean his nails with it as he looks at me and grins.

My hands begin to shake and a lump forms in my throat.

"I haven't seen anyone. Just like I told your friend."

The driver shrugs, then rolls up his window.

As I drive out of the parking lot, the car follows close behind.

"Hey," I whisper, "I don't know who the hell these guys are, but they look psycho and one of them has a knife. Not to mention, I think they're tailing us."

A quiet voice comes from the backseat. "They think I'm in here."

"Really? What in the hell should I do now?"

"I don't know," she answers calmly. "But I wouldn't stop if I were you."

"Hey, you know what? I only let you get in my car because I thought you were in danger."

"Is that the only reason?" She lets out a small laugh.

"What?"

"Nothing."

"Look, whatever your name is, I think I should drop you off at an open store or an all-night restaurant, where you'll be safe."

"I won't be safe."

I'm just about to answer her when I hear the revving of an engine behind me, and then feel a strong jolt as the blue car rams into my bumper. My hands clench the wheel tight and everything feels like it's going in slow-motion.

The girl in the back sits up, screams, then tilts her head back and laughs.

*What the hell is so funny? Is she nuts?*

I look in the side mirror and see that the car is still following. What in the hell did this girl do to these crazy thugs to make them so crazy?

We approach a set of lights. I look over at the all-night donut shop on the corner, and I'm just about to stop at the red light when I see a black and white car with a light bar on top pulling into the donut shop.

I quickly step on the gas and blow through the red light, then lay on the horn. The thugs behind me obviously haven't noticed the cops yet, because they tail me right through the intersection.

I look over at the police cruiser. It's booting it out of the parking lot and heading my way, fast. I slow down, causing the blue car to get even closer, and I draw a huge breath of relief when I hear the siren and see the bright blue and red lights flash.

Pulling over to the side of the road I watch as the blue car speeds past me, the cops in hot pursuit. Once they round the corner, I put my head on the steering wheel.

"Are you ok?" the girl says.

"Yeah. What the hell was that all about?" I say, my relief turning to anger.

She leans over the front seat, extends her hand to me, and says, "I'm Storm."

# Chapter Two

Dark clouds cast a dreary mood over the morning as the prison gates shrink in the rear-view mirror. Even though the deafening silence in the car is fueling my anxiety, it's nothing like the months of hell I've just lived through.

Time served—nine months in a cement jungle while my captors went to work at reprogramming my flawed character. My father, Clay Stewart, the reluctant chauffeur for my freedom ride, always before emanating a youthful presence, now has wide brush strokes of silver streaming through his brown hair and deep, severe lines around his eyes and mouth. A by-product of the stress brought on by the immense disappointment he feels over me—his only child.

On the ferry, I shuffle behind my father as he maneuvers through throngs of tourists and hunts for vacant seats. After some luck, we find two seats across from each other, and he predictably opens his newspaper and does his best to ignore me. Lines of people walk by, looking down at me as they pass. I slouch my shoulders and lower my gaze. An hour into the turbulent sailing, my father asks me if I'd like something to eat. I shake my head and he stuffs his paper under one arm, gets up, and walks down the aisle.

Looking out over the churning sea, I feel overwhelmed with hopelessness. I never thought I'd miss the six square meters of my cell. My mind escapes to a memory of when I was in a school play and my father was sitting proudly in the front row. The bright stage lights shone in my eyes and obscured most of the audience, but I could see my dad clearly, shoulders back and wearing an appreciative grin. I felt ten feet tall that day. That was a long time ago.

When the ship's whistle blows and the overhead message—"Thanks for travelling with BC Ferries"—plays, my father and I make our way back to the car deck. As we follow the traffic the ship, my dad turns on the radio. The song "My Girl" by The Temptations plays through the speakers. I immediately reach out and turn it off.

It's the song that Storm always hummed to me, and she's the last person that I need to be reminded of right now.

My father glares at me. "I was listening to that. Why did you shut it off?"

"I'm sorry. I just really can't stand that song."

He turns his attention back to the road, makes a few audible grumbles and then takes the north exit onto the Island Highway.

Thankfully, there's only another hour left of confined awkwardness before I get to see my mom—I've missed her desperately. The last time I saw her was about a year ago when she came over to Vancouver to buy supplies with the Logans, co-owners with my parents of the cabin resort. Other than that, I only make it home some Christmas's, depending on my father's mood.

The rest of the journey goes without incident—or interaction—between my father and me until finally we reach Merville, a small community of laid-back, good-natured islanders where my parents have lived and worked renting summer cabins for as long as I can remember. We take Tasman Road all the way to the seashore before turning into the lot.

The place looks much as it always has—six cabins in a horseshoe and the main office building off to the side. I look over at the weathered sign that reads *Stogan's Resort*, a combination of my parents' last name, Stewart, and the Logans'.

Despite the incomparable beauty of the area, I spent many of my younger years dreaming of the day when I'd be old enough to break away from here.

My father gets out, closes his door and walks toward the main building, leaving me to pop the trunk and retrieve my bag. Although I can't wait to see my mom, I'm dreading being holed up in the same house as my dad. A car ride is one thing but spending 24/7 in the same space is quite another.

As soon as I open my car door, a powerful gust of sea air pushes against me. I close my eyes and draw in a deep breath to give me strength for the confrontation I will undoubtedly face with my father, once he's had a few drinks. He's not normally a drinker, except for when he's stewing about something. Because of the embarrassment I've put him and my mother through, I'm almost positive he has a lot of pent-up aggression he'd just love to unleash on me. All he needs is some liquid courage— bourbon.

After grabbing my bag, I stop and gaze out over the endless sandbar, watching gulls fight against the wind as they struggle to land. The sky matches the sea, a grey monochrome color, making it hard to distinguish where one ends and the other begins. I watch as tall swells with white tips roll into shore. Throwing my bag over one shoulder, I turn and walk over to the main cabin.

The heavy wooden door creaks on its hinges when I open it. Inside, the familiar smell of percolating coffee and freshly baked bread permeates the air. I flop my bag down on a kitchen chair and start looking around for Mom. She's not in the living room, the biggest room in the house. My father knocked out a couple of walls and expanded the room so that travelers and tourists that were renting cabins could have a common area to meet. I never understood the draw of having a bunch of strangers hanging out in your private living area, but my parents are far more socially outgoing than I am.

I peek inside the laundry room and the large pantry before heading upstairs. About halfway up, I hear the music of Edit Piaf—my mother's favorite singer.

At the top of the stairwell, I look over and see my father sitting in his office in front of his wooden desk. He's looking at his computer screen. The floorboards creak under my feet and he briefly glances over at me, then looks away. I walk down the hall toward the music. My parent's bedroom door is only open a few inches, but the tunes coming from inside are blaringly loud, making it easy for me to go undetected. I slowly push the door open. My mom, a grey haired, lofty woman in her sixties, has her back to me and is bending over the bed, singing loudly out of tune while she folds a large pile of laundry.

I smile and walk softly into the room. She turns and sees me, and her mouth falls open. She quickly shuts off the music and then holds out her arms. "Paisley, you're here!"

It's obvious by her surprised reaction that she didn't hear us pull up and I guess my dad didn't let her know we had arrived—my father, the great communicator.

When I step closer and see her crystal-green eyes start to water, I muster every bit of strength in me not to cry. I have to be tough. I don't want her to see what that place did to me. It would hurt her too badly. I have to pretend that everything is ok, and I've come out of my experience unscathed. I hold my head high and pull my shoulders back. I walk into her arms and she squeezes me tightly, her chin on my shoulder. She sniffles, her chest vibrates, and she starts to cry.

I hold her firmly, running my hand up and down the back of her beige sweater. I'm keeping it together—so far. After a few moments, she pulls her head back and stares into my eyes. Suddenly, I feel myself starting to unravel, all of the horrible things I've seen and all of the pain I've been through since I saw her last rises to the surface. I don't have to say a word. By the way she is reading me, she knows it all. She reaches behind her for the bed while she keeps her eyes fixated on me and then sits, pulling me down beside her.

"It's ok, Paisley. It's over now, you're home," she says, her voice nurturing and soft. With all of my protective armor gone, I feel like I'm a little girl, safe and warm in her mother's arms. I try to choke back the tears but am unsuccessful. Every bit of pent up emotion pours out of my eyes. I lay my head on her lap as she strokes my hair.

"Mom, it was awful in there."

"I know, sweetie. I know. But you're home now and you can create a new beginning for yourself."

"But I'm nothing now. I'm worthless—an ex-con."

"No, Paisley. You never committed a crime, not intentionally. You're innocent and you're the same person that you've always been."

"It doesn't matter if I'm innocent or guilty, I have a criminal record now and that's what people care about."

"And it matters to you what people think? Really? This, coming from a girl that's gay?"

I laugh while still crying. "You have a point there."

Her warm, tender hands brush my cheek as she wipes away my tears.

"Mom, can I ask you something?" I look up at her. "Why didn't you come see me? Or even write?"

"I couldn't, Paisley."

"Because you were ashamed of me?"

"No. Because I knew if I did, you would have crumbled and you needed to be as strong and as resilient as you could be in there."

She knows me better than I know myself, and she's right. If she would've seen me in prison and I broke down, which I would have, the other inmates would target me as weak and vulnerable. Inside, you have to be tough, and if you aren't tough, you'd better be damn good at acting like you are.

"I understand, Mom," I say, lifting my head and wiping my eyes.

This time when I look at her, I notice the fine lines on her face. Her age is starting to show. Before I was sent away, she stopped dying her hair blond and let her natural grey come through. Regardless of how she's changed, she's a beautiful vision in front of me, a sense of home.

When we hear my father clear his throat, we both turn toward the door. I immediately straighten my back and draw in a deep breath. I avoid making eye contact with him. I don't want him to see my red eyes.

"Why didn't you tell me you were home, Clay?" my mother says, sounding a bit agitated.

"Because, Rose, that damn music you had on was so loud, you wouldn't have heard me. I knew you'd eventually figure out that we were here."

My mom shakes her head and sighs then turns to me. "Are you hungry?"

"Starving."

Just as we're leaving the room, I glance out of the window and see a tall, spindly man with grey, straggly hair walking in the lot.

"Is that Jasper?"

My mom smiles. "Yes. He's still working here."

Jasper has been a fixture here since way before my parents bought the place. He looked about a hundred years old when I was a small child. I can't believe he's still working here this many decades later.

"You'll have to say hello when you bump into him."

"Mom, he's the grumpiest, most anti-social guy on the planet. Even when I was little and I tried to talk to him, all he would do is grumble."

"Well, that's just his way. Underneath that tough exterior, he's got a good heart."

"Yeah, right." I say, shaking my head. "Does he still live in that little cabin up the woods?"

My mom nods, "Make sure you're pleasant to him, dear. He's a bit of a hermit but he's always been a very loyal worker."

We had dinner. It was thankfully quiet. The rest of the night went smoothly—my mother had 'accidentally' forgotten to buy my dad a bottle of bourbon.

# Chapter Three

When the morning sun streams into the room and onto my eyelids, I lie half asleep, waiting for the guards to walk into my room and tell me it's time to line up for head count. Then, I hear the faint sound of gulls. I sit up and look outside. It's going to be a beautiful day. The sky is blue with small puffs of unthreatening clouds.

I walk into the bathroom and stare at my pale skin and messy shoulder length blond hair. I am a disheveled mess. I grab my robe and open the door to the hallway, the welcoming aroma of coffee and bacon gifting me with the sense of home.

Just as I start walking down the stairs, I hear a rap at the front door and then my father inviting whomever it is inside. I make a face. The last thing I want to do is to see company. I quietly turn on the stairs and am just starting to tiptoe back up when my mother calls me from the foot of the stairs. "Paisley, I'm glad you're awake. The Logans are here to see you."

Lily and Ren Logan have been my parents' best friends since before I was born. Usually, wherever my parents are, the Logans aren't far behind. I don't mind them, other than Ren's annoying habit of sniffing after he says something—after a while it starts to grate on my nerves. Both Ren and Lily are around the same age as my parents. They were both schoolteachers until they bought into our resort and became partners.

Lily has bright auburn hair and unlike Mom she is slim, with an athletic build. Ren has grey hair with a huge bald spot in the back. He's slim too, if you don't count his half a basketball-sized belly. They are far more open minded and non-judgmental than my dad and whenever there's a subject that my father opposes, the Logans are quick to debate him. I've always liked listening to their diplomatic and civil disputes. The Logans do what I never have the balls to do. They stand up to my father.

I think the only thing that I don't admire about them is their do-good, snotty daughter, Ivy. She's been a pain in my ass since we first started school together. I think both the Logan's and my parents hoped that we would be best friends—that never happened. Instead, we were opposites. I had human friends, Ivy had robotic clones, following her around the school. It made me sick. What pisses me off even more is how liberal and open-minded her parents are. Ivy can talk to them about anything—they never judge her.

A few years ago, Ivy came out as gay to her parents. I remember being so shocked when my mom told me. Although Ivy was always pretty, in a Barbie kind of way, she was a snob, always looking down on everyone else. I just couldn't imagine her being a lesbian, or at least admitting to it. I always thought that Ivy would grow up, marry a doctor or a lawyer, have 2.5 kids and be the president of the PTA. She just gave off that conventional, predictable vibe.

When she first told her parents that she was a lesbian, all her mom and dad did was praise her for her strength to come forward. No shit! Meanwhile, when my dad found a Penthouse magazine under my bed, he demanded that my mom take me to my doctor because there was undoubtedly something wrong with my head.

\* \* \*

Reluctantly, I walk down the stairs and follow my mother into the kitchen. As soon as I enter the room, the Logans stand and take turns hugging me. They look me up and down, searching for badly done tattoos or scars from fighting until they're satisfied that I am, in fact, the same person I have always been, at least on the outside.

After I pour a coffee, I sit down at the table, waiting for the uncomfortable questions about my *plans for the future* to begin. I can't help but wonder what my parents have told them about the events that led to my incarceration, or about Storm. How she set me up and broke my heart.

The first predictable question comes from Lily, who asks me if I'm planning on continuing

my career as an accountant. I have no idea—
how many people are going to trust their
company's books and money to an ex-con?
After a shoulder shrug and a smile, it's obvious
to everyone that I haven't a bloody clue what
direction my life might take. Suddenly, I'm
painfully aware that I'm a twenty-seven-year-
old screw-up with nothing but a rap sheet and
emotional problems.

Thankfully, Ren takes the focus off me.
"Have you heard that Ivy became a writer?" he
says, grinning proudly.

"Really? That's amazing," I answer, trying
to sound interested.

"She's been writing a column for the Island
Newspaper," adds Lily.

*What's the column about? How to be an
asshole?*

I nod and smile. "Wow, good for her."

My mother nudges me and says, "Don't
you want to know what her column is about?"

"Of course, I do. That was my next
question." *No, it wasn't.*

Ren tells me that Ivy has a weekly column
about health and beauty tips. *I'm going to gag.*

"Gee, that doesn't surprise me at all," I say,
using every bit of my junior acting skills to
sound thrilled.

"Speaking of Ivy," says Ren. "Have your
parents told you the big news yet?"

"Big news?" I ask. My mom immediately
looks down, telling me that I may not find the
so-called 'big news' very appealing.

My father leans over and folds his hands together on the table. "The four of us are going away for a month and you and Ivy are going to be in charge of the place until we get back."

"What?" I say the word much louder than intended.

My father shoots me an unimpressed look. "That's right, Paisley. The resort will be closed while we're in Florida, so all you have to do is answer phones and do some prep work around the grounds and in the cabins. Jasper is doing all of the maintenance, so your job shouldn't be too hard."

Me and Ivy? Are they nuts? The last time we were together was about ten years ago. I had wanted to stay in one of the cabins with a few of my friends, but Ivy, the prima donna, had taken up the only two vacant cabins for her and her stupid clones. Long story short, a huge fight broke out, ending with Ivy and me rolling around, trying to kill each other. Our parents are nuts if they think this whole stupid plan of theirs is going to work.

I excuse myself from the table and walk back up to the bedroom. My mother is only a minute behind me. As I sit on the bed, she raps on the door and walks in. "Paisley, I know you're upset about Ivy coming. I get it. But she's the only one who knows how to operate this place while we're not here."

"How hard is it to answer the phone?"

"There's more to taking care of the office and cabins than that. She's worked here every summer since she was a kid."

"I just wish that I didn't have to be here at the same time."

"But you do, Paisley." She gives me a sad smile. "Part of your parole conditions are that you are working here and aren't around any bad influences."

"This is so bloody ridiculous."

As Mom and I sit on the bed, we hear someone at the front door. It doesn't take long before I recognize Ivy's high-pitched voice. "Sonofabitch," I say, flopping backward onto the bed.

My mother pats my leg. "We're not leaving for a couple of days yet. We'll make sure everything is running smoothly before we go."

When she leaves the room, I stare out the window. As much as prison sucked, it was home for nine months. Here, I don't feel like I belong. I never did. Even though there were unbearable elements of living in an institution—the bullies, like Violet, and the lack of freedom—at least I didn't have to deal with the tension between my father and me.

And I certainly didn't have to see Ivy.

* * *

After I'm dressed, I stay in my room for as long as possible, avoiding the inevitable reunion

24

with Ivy. After about an hour, my father yells for me to come downstairs.

Reluctantly I meander to the living room, where everyone is sitting and chatting. As soon as I walk into the room, I see her: the prim and pretentious Ivy.

Her hair is slicked back into a tight, perfect chignon and her makeup is perfect. She's wearing a pink, two-piece skirt and blazer set and a matching silk scarf around her neck. The sight of her instantly makes my stomach tighten as I remember everything I've always hated about her.

The topic of discussion is her—just the way she likes it. Everyone asks her about her writing, her friends and what new products she's promoting in her column. I do my best not to nod off. Seeing my immense boredom and no doubt sensing my immense disapproval of the pink queen, my mother asks me to make coffee and get cookies for everyone. I'm useless in the kitchen but since I'm not being asked to cook anything, I jump at the chance to escape the room.

As I'm measuring the grounds and putting them in the filter, I see a flash of pink in the reflection of the coffee maker. Oh great, it's followed me.

"Hello, Miss Priss. Nice outfit."

"A little overdressed, I know." Her voice is cool. "But I wanted to look nice for this little get-together. Or should I say, pity party?"

I turn to look at her. "Whatever, Ivy. Only an idiot would dress like that and come to a rustic resort on the beach."

"You know what? You're right," she says, glancing at my grey sweats and t-shirt. "I was actually going to wear what you have on, but Walmart wasn't open yet."

My mom hollers from the next room: "How are you girls making out in there?"

"Did she just ask us how we are 'making out'?" she says, grabbing cups from the cupboard. "You should be so lucky,"

"Oh please, Ivy. I wouldn't touch you with my enemy's lips."

The coffee seems to take forever as we stand silently and wait. Thankfully, both of us have run out of insults to hurl at each other. When the drinks and cookies are on the tray, I carry them to the living room—I wouldn't want Barbie to get anything on her diva clothes. Everyone talks idly about current events in their lives while I look out of the window and let my mind take me away to somewhere other than here—a place that's peaceful and has less pink in it.

\* \* \*

Settled on the bed with my elbows resting on the windowsill, I stare out over the cove. A full moon casts a shining path of light over the water. Usually when she finds her way into my thoughts, I can chase her away, but not tonight.

Tonight, I'm feeling vulnerable and alone—the perfect mental environment for memories of Storm to haunt me.

I never knew someone so beautiful existed until the night I first laid eyes on her. Her long, dark, wet hair framed her flawless complexion so perfectly. And those lips—so full and inviting. I wanted her from the second I first saw her, and she knew it. I would do anything for her. She knew that, too.

I guess that's why it was so easy for her to manipulate me, to use me to get whatever she wanted. But her power over me didn't only stem from her beauty. Storm was wild and fearless—the complete opposite of me. I remember her doing things that I could never do, daring things like taking off her shirt in a movie theatre and then waiting to see how long it took before people noticed. She got off on the attention she garnered, even if it was bad. There was nothing she wouldn't do. Over the three months we spent together, I saw her pickpocket a cop who was struggling with a homeless man, eat at a fancy courtyard café and then run like hell to avoid paying—I even watched her take off her shoes in Holt Renfrew and put on new ones, leaving her old pair in their place. I knew the things she did were wrong, but I did nothing, I couldn't. I was completely smitten by her.

Sometimes, she could be mean. I saw her get into a lot of fights—sometimes in a bar or even just walking through a crowd. It didn't take much to set her off. I don't think I ever witnessed her hit someone that deserved it. She would have these crazy moments that were completely random. Still, I followed her everywhere.

I hear the water running in the hallway and then stop. The noise brings me back to my current reality, in a place where I don't belong. I have to get out of here, even just for a while. After my parents are in bed, I tip-toe down the stairs and out the front door.

* * *

I walk gently across the gravel to avoid being heard by my father—even though their bedroom is on the second floor, he's the lightest sleeper I've ever known.

As soon as I reach the tall grass just before the beach, I kick off my slippers and leave them where they're easy to find when I come back. The moon illuminates the seafoam as it crawls up the shore, making the edges of the water appear neon. As soon as my feet hit the cool sand, I feel free. I'm out of view of the cabins and my parents' watchful eye and here, under the glowing full moon, and for the first time in nine months, I am completely alone. Finally.

I stroll down to the water's edge, my feet leaving prints in the soft sand. As I look out over the shimmering water, I wish I were a bird, able to fly above the beautiful ocean or over the majestic mountains in the distance. As long as I didn't have to be here right now - or be me.

When I've spent about an hour walking up and down the shoreline, I decide to lie on a beached log and look up at the sky. I'll have to go back to the house soon. Someone might get up in the night and if I'm not in my room, all hell will break out. I close my eyes tightly and then open them. Millions of bright stars shine in the dark sky. I do my best not to think about my father, the fact that I feel lost or even how tormented I feel about Storm. Instead, I take deep breaths and imagine that I'm a part of everything around me, the wind that brushes over me or the waves that sound like music playing in the distance.

* * *

I wake to my body being rocked briskly by my shoulder. When I open my eyes, I see Jasper standing over me. I quickly sit up and look around. I'm still here at the beach, except all the stars and the moon have disappeared and made way for the morning sun that is approaching fast over the horizon.

"I must have dozed off out here last night," I say, making embarrassed eye contact with the grey old man.

"Not my care. But you'd better get yourself back up to the main cabin before your parents get up," he says, before turning and heading back up toward the cabins.

I quickly rub my face, stand up and focus. I'm so grateful that Jasper woke me. If he didn't and my father saw that I wasn't in the house, he probably wouldn't even look for me—he'd just call the cops and report me missing.

Once back in the main house, I repeat the same process as I did when I snuck out last night. I tip-toe across the wooden floor then quietly up the stairs, making sure not to wake anyone. As soon as the door to the bedroom is closed and I'm sitting on my bed, I breathe a sigh of relief, *Thanks, Jasper. I owe you one.*

By the time my parents are up and are making noise downstairs in the kitchen, I've already had my shower, done my hair and gotten dressed to go see the parole officer in Courtenay later. I get downstairs just as my dad is walking out the front door. He pretends not to hear me as it closes.

Mom has her back to me as she stands over a sizzling frying pan on the stove. She notices me when I walk up beside her and grab a coffee mug out of the cupboard.

"How did you sleep?" she says in her happy morning tone.

"Great, thanks. Do you want help making breakfast?"

"No thanks, just get your coffee and grab a seat. It's almost ready. We'll eat when your father gets back."

"Where did he go?"

"To the beach to get a bucket of sand to keep by the fireplace."

"Why?"

"Oh, you know your father. He's a worrywart. He just wants to make sure that if you girls have a fire when we're away, there's sand nearby."

"He's getting more paranoid in his old age, you know that, right?"

She shrugs and winks then resumes cooking.

After a few moments, I hear the front door open and then the sound of Dad kicking off his boots. He walks into the kitchen and makes his way over to his chair at the head of the table. I barely look up. Then, I hear a thwack as he slaps something down in front of him. I lift my head and at the same time my mother turns to see what the noise is. There in front of him are both of my sand-covered slippers.

"Get those off the table," my mother says.

My father's eyes meet mine. "Why were these near the beach?"

"I don't know," I say, lowering my gaze to my coffee. "Maybe they got restless last night and went for a walk."

"Don't be a smartass, Paisley."

I feel something inside me snap. Suddenly, I find myself talking to him in a way I never have. "Are you seriously questioning why my slippers were outside?" I meet his gaze again. "They're obviously there because I went to the beach last night. So what? Is that a crime?"

"It's funny you should mention crime."

"Please stop it, you two," my mom says, dishing food onto plates.

31

I pretend I don't hear her. Instead, I stare hard at my father. How dare he insinuate that I'm a criminal. My pent-up anger and pain boil under my skin.

"Can't we just have a nice relaxing breakfast to start our day?" my mom says, placing our food in front of us.

"I don't know, Dad. Can we?"

"What were you doing out so late? Meeting someone?"

"Yeah, Dad. I waited for you and Mom to go to bed, then I called the prison on the mainland and got a few girls to break out of jail. They swam across the straight so we could meet on the beach and do criminal things together."

"Stop it!" Mom yells, her voice shaking and threatening tears.

"Who knows what kind of person you turned into in prison. I've heard all about how people get hooked on drugs in those places."

"There is something so backward about your thinking. Thanks for the vote of confidence, Father."

He shakes his head then turns his attention to his food. I can't believe him. Does he really believe the bullshit that just spewed out of his mouth? It makes no sense. Is he insinuating that all prisoners are drug addicts? What a bunch of bullshit. I never touched street drugs once, before or after I was in prison. He watches way too much TV.

My mom is visibly shaken as she struggles to eat. A mixed cocktail of guilt and anger rises up in my throat, making it impossible to have my meal. I slowly stand up, grab my plate and walk to the counter. After placing my food beside the sink, I walk over to where my mom is sitting and touch her shoulder. "I'm sorry. I'll eat later. I just need to go to my room."

She nods without saying anything.

In my room, I start to think about how the hell I'm going to survive here. I left this place because I couldn't breathe anymore. My father had sucked every bit of oxygen out of this house and I could barely move. When I did disobey him and stay out past my curfew or whatever else young people do, he would scrutinize and demean me for days. In some ways, living here was more like prison than doing real time in an institution.

I lie on the bed and take myself through a relaxation regime that I learned from a therapist when I was doing time. Slow breathing, peaceful visualizations and blocking bad thoughts. Just when I feel like I can drift off to sleep, a temporary escape, my mother knocks on the door and walks in.

"Oh, sorry, dear. Were you sleeping?"

I shake my head and sit up.

She sits beside me and smiles. "I know that you have an appointment with your parole officer in a couple of hours, but your father and I have so much work to do before we leave tomorrow so Ivy has agreed to drive you."

That was it. The topping to my already shitty morning. I sigh and flop backwards on the bed.

"Oh, don't be so bummed. Maybe it's time for you and Ivy to bury the hatchet."

"The only way I want to bury the hatchet with Ivy is in the back of her head."

"Don't say such things, dear." My mom pats my leg and leaves the room.

Great. Just when I thought things couldn't get any worse, now I have to drive all the way into Courtenay with Shallow Barbie.

* * *

Staring at the dated green and beige wallpaper of my bedroom, a familiar sensation starts to rise in me—coldness. I think it's a defense mechanism that involuntarily occurs when I'm in a situation I can do nothing about, when I am defenseless. I've never been one to suffer with depression, even when I was incarcerated. But here in this room, as I look my bleak future in the face, I'm feeling something dark and scary trying to grab a hold of me. Coldness is one thing, it makes me more resilient, but this new feeling I'm experiencing is scary. I'm going to have to try hard to avoid succumbing to it.

When I hear Ivy's irritating voice coming from the downstairs foyer, it sends a shiver up my back. I don't answer. I don't move. Then, my father calls me, and I know if I don't respond, he'll stomp up the stairs and come into the room. Fearing another confrontation, I get up and unenthusiastically slog my way down the stairs.

Ivy is standing at the foot of the stairs. Today, she's wearing blue jeans and a collared shirt with a tweed blazer and a neck scarf. The scarf is a maroon color, as are her shoes. I guess this is her attempt at dressing casual—fail. I follow her as she turns and walks outside.

An older model 5 series convertible BMW sits in the driveway, obviously hers. I'm relieved to see it's black and not pink. As soon as we get in, a thick waft of heavy perfume hits me. I cough and sputter as I unwind my window.

"What's your problem?" she asks, checking her hair in the mirror.

"Are you serious? Your perfume is so thick, I can barely breathe. I don't know how you can stand it."

"Shut up, Paisley!"

"I'm serious. That stench is so thick in here, I can literally taste it."

"Well at least I don't use old man's Irish Spring soap," she retorts. "You smell like a pine-tree air freshener."

"Ivy, I'm not kidding. You are going to have to take the roof down on this thing or I'll never make the trip."

"I can barely smell my perfume, and nobody else I go around says anything about it."

"That's because the stench is so powerful it messes with their brain and renders them speechless."

Ivy starts the car and looks over at me. "Don't even think of putting your feet on the dash!"

"Why? My shoes are probably worth more than this car is."

"Nice try. Just don't do it."

"Ok, Stinky, whatever you say."

When we stop in Merville to get gas, I walk inside the station. Thankfully, Ivy takes the top down before pumping the fuel. *Maybe she caught a whiff of herself and couldn't stand it either.* While I wait, I peruse postcards beside the till. After a couple of minutes, Ivy walks in and up to the cashier, a kindly lady in her mid-forties. When Ivy asks how much she owes, I walk up beside her to pay.

The cashier tells Ivy she needs twenty bucks for the gas. I reach in my pocket, pull out a twenty-dollar bill and hand it to the clerk. Ivy quickly snatches it out of the woman's hand and passes the bill back to me.

"Use my money, Ivy. You're driving me to an appointment. I'll pay for the gas."

"You don't need to. Your mom already gave me cash."

"Are you bloody kidding me? My mom paid you for driving me?"

"Kind of pathetic, don't you think?"

And I thought I couldn't feel any more demoralized than I did back at the house—was I ever wrong. I leave the building in a huff, dragging whatever is left of my pride behind me.

When we're back on the road, Ivy turns on the stereo. Pop music blares over the speakers. I lean forward and turn the volume down. Ivy turns it back up. I shoot her an angry look before turning it down again. This time, she turns the dial all the way to maximum, deafening me with crappy bubble-gum music. She looks at me and smirks, then starts bopping her head to the beat. I scowl back at her as I grab the dial, turn down the music, then pull the dial off and throw it out the window.

Ivy gasps and quickly looks in the rear-view mirror to see if it's safe to pull over—it's not. There is a line of cars behind us.

"You are going to pay for that, Paisley! Or maybe you won't have to. Maybe your mom will pay for you."

"Shut your mouth, Ivy, or I'll shut it for you."

We stop talking until we arrive in Courtenay. Then, Ivy pulls over to the side of the road to check Maps so she can find directions to the parole office. After she figures out how to get there, we are just about to pull back out onto the road when a red pick up pulls up next to us. A guy in his mid-forties is sitting behind the wheel. He's wearing a tacky rayon purple shirt and a baseball cap. He looks down into the car and grins. "Hey, hotties, where's the party?"

Just then, Ivy's phone rings. She answers it as the trucker says loudly, "So, are you girls from here?"

Ivy looks at him and then looks back at me. "What did he say?"

"He said he hates your hair, and he can smell you from there."

She gives me a nasty look then continues speaking into her phone.

"You girls wanna get a drink somewhere?" the pick-up artist says.

I lean over Ivy. "Hey," I holler, "you know when you meet someone and there's this electricity between you?"

"Yeah," he says, trying to sound suave.

"Well, none of that is happening here. The only thing we feel for you is disgust."

"Is that right?"

"That's right, my friend. I would not lie to you."

"Well maybe your friend feels differently?"

"First of all, she's not my friend. Secondly, I'm almost positive that you're wasting your time."

"You're a bitch," he says before speeding away.

I laugh to myself just as Ivy gets off her phone and looks at me. "What did he want?'

"He wanted to pay me fifteen bucks to go on a date with you. I didn't want to over-charge him, so I agreed to ten and told him I'd drop you off at his motel in an hour."

"As if, Paisley."

"I don't know what you're so pissed about. I just made you ten bucks. Just think of all the cheap makeup you can buy with that."

"I swear, I regret the hell out of agreeing to drive you to your stupid appointment. Maybe in the future you'll want to think about the burden you put on everyone else. Maybe that will make you think twice before landing your ass back in jail."

\* \* \*

The parole office is located in a strip mall, kitty corner to a busy four-way stop. In a small town like Courtenay, it wouldn't take long before you were spotted entering the shameful place. After that, it would only be a matter of time before everyone was talking about it. At least in Vancouver people stick to themselves, maybe too much so. Other than going to work and a quick stop to get groceries, I never left my apartment. I had been in my suite for five years and never said more than two words to my neighbors, or them to me. I'm not sure what's worse, complete seclusion in a big city or having everyone knowing your business in a small town.

Ivy sits in the car and fixes her hair while I go into the office, check in and then take a seat on a hard metal chair by the window. After a while, I hear a door open in the hallway behind the desk. Soon, a thin, scraggly dressed man in dirty worn clothes comes out, a little girl about five walking beside him and holding his hand. He walks up to the counter and tells the clerk that he wants to make another appointment in a week. As the woman behind the desk taps away on her computer, the little girl starts pulling at the man's shirt and whining—she is restless and tired of waiting for him.

The man tries to talk to the clerk and settle on an appointment time, but the child persists. I watch, fully expecting the man to get upset with the child and tell her to sit down and be quiet, he doesn't. Instead, he shifts his attention from the receptionist then leans down and speaks softly to the little girl, assuring her that they'll be on their way soon. A few moments later, the clerk hands the man an appointment confirmation card and the man and the girl leave. I watch through the window as the duo walk down the sidewalk, he's smiling at her and she's smiling back. I can't help but get a warm feeling and a bit of jealousy as I witness their connection. If a man like this, a man way down on his luck, can put his own issues aside to show his daughter love, why can't my father try to put even a little effort into our relationship?

"Paisley, you can come with me," the receptionist says.

I get up and follow her down the narrow corridor to a small room with a desk and a loveseat in it. A large, generic picture of flowers is on the longest wall, while small plaques with awards, accolades or acknowledgements are strewn over the remaining three. There is a clinical, frigid feeling about this place—then again, I can't see why they would spend the time or effort making it feel cozy and welcoming. This is not a community friendship place, it's a place of rules and obedience.

I'm feeling fidgety and restless, kind of like the little girl was out front. Like her, all I want to do is get out of here. I have never seen a probation officer before and I have no idea what to expect. All I know is that I'm worried about what they'll say or what regulations they will slap on me. Either way I'm going to be seen as guilty, as usual. I'm getting really tired of professing my innocence and defending myself.

When she walks into the room, I'm both shocked and relieved. I was expecting a lawyer-type man, staunch and closed off. Instead, a kindly woman with disheveled long hair and sun-drenched skin walks in. Her pants and flowy shirt look like they were bought in the sixties. She immediately extends her hand and shakes mine. "Hi, I'm Chloe. You must be Paisley?" She sits on the loveseat beside me. In her hand is a thin green folder.

She asks me basic questions: where I'm living, who my parents are and how I'm feeling now that I'm out of prison. Next, she opens the file and scans down the black type on the page. She nods as she reads. After a few quick moments, she closes the folder and looks at me.

"Let me see if I've got things right. You were an accountant. You met a girl, one that is known to police. You fell hard for this person and she used your affection to take advantage of you. Then she had you move a bag with drugs, paraphernalia and guns and when the cops showed up, she took off and let you take the fall?"

"Does it say all that in that file?" I ask, feeling surprised.

"Not all of it. But it's what I read between the lines."

"Damn, you're good," I say, smiling.

"I've been doing this work since you were in diapers," she says with a laugh. Then she turns serious. "So, why didn't you give her up to the cops? I'm sure with your help, they could've caught her and thrown her in jail instead of you."

"I know this sounds stupid but, I couldn't rat her out. It's not my style." I look down at my hands. "In a way, I guess I felt like I deserved to be punished because I was stupid enough to trust her. Plus, at the time, I thought she loved me. For the first couple of months, I expected her to come forward and tell the truth. As you can see, she never did."

"I'm sorry this happened to you, Paisley. You seem like a nice person, but you can't blame yourself. I would probably do the same thing in your position. We all want to believe in the good in people. Unfortunately, we can be let down and disappointed sometimes."

Chloe is amazing. She's kind, honest and nonjudgmental. For the first time in a long time, I feel vindicated and less guilty. After we talk awhile longer, I ask her how frequently I'll need to meet with her. I wouldn't mind if it was every few days. At least here, nobody is suspicious of my intentions, like my father is.

Chloe tells me that because I always tested negative for drugs while I was incarcerated and because of the nature of my case, she believes that I am low risk, therefore, she only needs to see me every month. Although I'm grateful that she believes in my innocence and trusts me, I feel a bit disappointed that I won't be seeing her more often.

At the end of our meeting, we both stand up. She pats my shoulder and says, "Hang in there. Things will get better. You'll get your life back. I have no doubt."

\* \* \*

By the time I get back to the car, Ivy has nodded off with her head resting against the window. Instead of making a loud noise or shocking her—my first instinct—I'm feeling too happy to take advantage of her vulnerability right now, regardless if she's my enemy. I want to stay in my newly found happy bubble for as long as I can.

# Chapter Four

On the way home, Ivy tries to get under my skin by playing the most annoying commercial pop on the radio, but it doesn't bother me. I'm too busy feeling great, reminiscing about how well the parole meeting just went. Time passes quickly and before I know it, we're back at the resort.

When we're parked, I start to thank Ivy for the ride, but she pretends she doesn't hear me. She gets out of the car and walks to the main house without a word. Jerk.

As soon as I walk in the door, my mom hollers from the kitchen, "How was your meeting?"

I kick off my shoes and walk into the room. Dad is sitting down with Ivy and Mom is putting snacks on the table. I take a seat, grab a saucer and start loading my plate.

"The meeting went very well, Mom. Thanks for asking."

Ivy takes her cell out of her purse and starts texting. My father is preoccupied with the food as he assembles meat and cheese on crackers and doesn't look up.

"So, when do you have to go back?" my mom asks.

"Actually, I won't have to go very often. Because I'm low risk, I'll only have to check in once a month."

My father scoffs and continues eating. My mother grabs the plate of pickles and hands them to me, clearly hoping to distract me from my father's insolence. As usual, she's trying to prevent conflict.

Putting the pickles down, I look over at my father. "I'm sorry, Dad. Did you have an opinion on what I was saying?"

For a few moments, he says nothing, he just keeps on eating. I stare at him, waiting for a reply. My mom makes noises shuffling things around the table, trying to break the tension.

Then, as if arriving at an answer, my dad says, "So, this parole officer, who doesn't know you, said you were low risk? What is he, psychic?"

Again, the rage doesn't allow me to stay silent. "He's a she, and no she's not psychic. She's been doing her job a long time and after reading my file and talking with me, she had a great understanding of my situation. I like her a lot. Do you know why?"

He doesn't answer or look at me.

"I like her because she didn't judge me. Instead, she gave me hope that I can get my life together again. It was really nice talking to someone who has faith in me, even if it was a stranger."

"Well, she hasn't had to live for the past nine months with a daughter in prison, has she?"

"Yeah, I can't imagine how hard that must have been for you, Dad. Even though I was the one doing the time. And you're forgetting the important fact that I was fucking innocent."

"Paisley, language, please!" my mother says.

I push my plate to the side and take a deep breath.

"I really wish you two wouldn't argue," she continues, her voice shaking slightly. "We're going away in the morning and you shouldn't part on a bad note, especially in front of company." She glances at Ivy.

"Don't worry, Mom," I say, getting up from the table. "Ivy is preoccupied with texting her plastic friends. I bet she can't even hear us."

I grab my plate, apologize to Mom for the outburst and am just heading for the door when Ivy blurts out, "I heard every word."

"Good," I answer as I leave the kitchen.

\* \* \*

As a sea breeze gusts through the open window, the sunlight shines through the fluttering curtains and dances on the patterned walls. Today is the day my parents and the Logans leave for Florida. I'll no longer be under my father's scrutiny and I can exist in peace.

That being said, I still have to contend with Ivy, but that shouldn't be too hard. This place is big enough that I'm sure we can stay in our perspective corners without tearing each other's heads off.

Sounds of clunking, zipping and packing emanate from my parents' room as my mom hurries to stow items of clothing and essentials into suitcases. I get up and stand in front of their open bedroom door. Mom has an armful of items and is looking down at an overstuffed suitcase.

"Need some help?" I ask, chuckling.

"I think we need to buy new luggage and throw these old rickety ones away," she says, shaking her head.

"Let me guess, Dad wouldn't spring for new ones?"

She looks at me and shakes her head.

After I've helped her stow more items into the bag, I wheel it downstairs as she walks behind me carrying two shoulder bags, a garment bag and a toiletry kit. I glance back at her, "Gee Mom. Are you taking everything you own?"

At the bottom of the stairwell is a mountain of matching red cases, Lily looking dwarfed behind them.

"See? I don't have near as much stuff as Lily does," Mom says, sounding validated.

I help the ladies to the Logans' van with all of their luggage. Ren is standing at the back of his vehicle, tossing each case in when my father walks up, takes everything out of the back of the van and insists on repacking it himself. By the time he's finished, the van will look like a moving container—everything systematically placed in a logical spot. It's annoying as hell, though Ren is so passive and easygoing, he gladly steps back and lets my controlling father take over.

After standing around and talking to my mom and the Logans for about twenty minutes, Ivy pulls in. My dad informs everyone that the van is packed and ready to go. I hug my Mom and the Logans and wish them well on their trip while my father avoids the sentimental goodbyes and opts for a quick smile and nod in my direction. Mom hands me a list of what to do around the resort. Then, she tells me that my father has left a list of prep work I should do to get things ready for Jasper's renos.

After everyone is loaded and buckled in the van, Ivy and I stand by and wait until they leave the driveway. Then Ivy goes to the back of her car and pulls out a monstrously enormous suitcase. She grunts and groans as she drags it to the main cabin.

"What's in there, your makeup?"

"No, you idiot. It's my clothes for the next month. Unlike you, I have a variety of outfits, not just one or two to choose from."

"I don't care, Ivy. What I do care about is why you're bringing that in the house."

"Because I'll be staying here for the next month."

"What? Are you kidding? Everyday?" My stomach forms a hard lump.

"That's right. I promised our parents that I would."

"That's ridiculous. You have your own home. You don't have to stay all the way out here. As a matter of a fact, you don't even have to come out here. I can just tell our parents that you did."

"Forget it. I gave my word. Plus, I've been working here every summer since I was a kid. I know this place way better than you do. If I wasn't here, you'd probably let everything go to shit."

I hate her. I really do. I walk in the kitchen, grab a bag of cookies and head upstairs. As soon as I'm in my room, I slam the door and then flop out on the bed. It doesn't take three minutes before Barbie-From-Hell is knocking at my door.

"Piss off, Ivy."

"Just so you know, I've made a list of tasks for both of us. I'm sliding your copy under the door."

What the hell is with everyone and their bloody lists?

Annoyed, I get off the bed and am just about to open the door to tell her where she can stick her list, when a small piece of paper appears under the door.

"Thanks, Ivy. I was running low on toilet paper."

I grab the list and crumble it up, then toss it into the wastebasket on my way back to the bed.

It's near 3PM when I wake up—I've slept half the day away. I don't mind, though. For the first time since arriving here, I feel relaxed.

I quickly wash my face and go downstairs to make a cup of tea, hoping to hell that Princess Ivy has gone out. As soon as I reach the bottom of the stairs, I hear noise coming from the kitchen. When I push the door open and walk in, Ivy is standing by the counter with my mother's recipe book open. I move around her, grab a tea bag and a cup from the cupboard and walk over to the sink.

"I'm making a roast for dinner."

"Good for you."

"I expect you to eat it, Paisley."

"Dream on," I say, pouring water in my cup before putting it in the microwave.

After the minute and a half it takes to heat my drink, I grab the cup, discard the teabag and start to leave the room when I look at the table and see a small, frozen hunk of meat. "Is that the roast?"

"Of course. What else would it be?"

"I'm no chef, but isn't it supposed to be thawed before you cook it?"

"How the hell should I know? But I think if it cooked at a hot enough temperature, it should—"

"Bye. Don't care," I interrupt, leaving the kitchen.

I'm the world's worst cook, a claim to fame I'm not proud of. I've just never been the domestic type. If I can't make it in the microwave, I order take-out. And, if memory serves me correctly, eight or so years ago Ivy brought a dish she made over for Christmas dinner—I think it was supposed to be a fruit crumble—that ended up being a burned on the outside, raw on the inside science experiment. Nobody ate it. No wonder she's so skinny— there's no take-out joints around here.

As I carry my tea on to the porch, the warm sea air rushes over me. I stand and watch the drifting waves as the wind blows through the tall Douglas firs that surround the cabins. I breathe in deeply and as I exhale, a calmness comes over me—I'm so happy that everyone's gone. Well, everyone except Ivy. But maybe after she gives herself food poisoning from eating one of her toxic concoctions, she'll have to go home and recover, the best-case scenario.

When I've finished my drink, I decide to go upstairs and find Dad's list of jobs so I can decide in what order to do things. One thing about this place: if you don't have something to do, it can get pretty boring, pretty fast. Staying occupied will be good for my brain, as well. I'll be able to gain some clarity so I can start figuring out what my long-term plans will be.

As soon as I open the door to my dad's office, I see Ivy sitting at his desk. "What are you doing in here?" I ask.

"Working. Why? Did you lose a bag of cookies or something?"

"Shut up. I'm supposed to get a list my dad wrote for me."

Ivy looks through a pile of papers in front of her before grabbing a sheet, reading it and then passing it to me.

I go downstairs to the common room, sit on the sofa and turn on the TV. There's literally nothing on, so I turn on my parents' ancient stereo and thumb through a stack of vintage records. I stop looking when I find a copy of *Herb Alpert, Whipped Cream & Other Delights*. As soon as I put the record on and turn up the volume, Miss Kill-Joy marches down the stairs, folds her arms and yells for me to turn it down. I point to my ears and shrug while I mouth the words, "Sorry, can't hear you."

I close my eyes while I sink into the sofa. The music sparks memories of when I was very young and my dad would sing along with these songs while I stood on his feet and hung onto his legs, dancing around the room together. I was his snuggle bunny and he was my superhero. I thought we would always have that unbreakable bond between us. I was so wrong. As soon as I grew up and veered off the path that he had mapped out for me, including being straight, then he distanced himself. With the lack of involvement from him, my mom stepped up and filled not only her part as a parent, but his too.

I think because of his indifference to me, I've never felt good enough for anyone's love. I guess that's why I was such an easy mark for Storm. I was vulnerable and insecure. In jail, I spoke to a counselor who told me how a lot of inmates end up on dark paths because of their low self-worth, usually stemming from dysfunction when they were growing up. As much as there were women that were hard cases in prison, there were also some girls that seemed gentle, lost and fragmented.

When the record finishes, I decide to go upstairs to take a shower, but as I turn off the stereo, the smoke alarm comes on. Almost instantly, I smell something putrid and thick. I walk to the bottom of the stairs. Light wisps of smoke creep out from below the kitchen door.

Oh no, what has that idiot done? As soon as I swing the door open, I see a cloud of smoke billowing from the oven. I yell for Ivy, then run and open the front door. Back in the kitchen, I shut the oven off and open the windows. Ivy bursts into the kitchen.

"What did you do?" she screams.

I shake my head and tell her to get a broom. She hands it to me, and I push the button on the fire detector. After the annoying alarm is off and I've fanned the smoke out of the windows using a tea towel, I sit down at the table to catch my breath.

"What happened?" Ivy asks.

"You cooked."

She walks over to the oven and peers inside before grabbing oven mitts and pulls out the burnt offering.

"Let me guess, dinner?"

"Whatever, Paisley. At least I made an attempt."

"You really shouldn't have. What a waste of food."

"No, it's not. I'll put it outside. The wild animals will eat it."

"I'm pretty sure they won't."

* * *

I spend the next few hours going over my father's list, deciding which tasks should be done first. When my eyes grow tired, I make a quick bowl of microwavable KD and then head to bed. At the top of the stairs, I open the linen closet door and grab a spare pillow. Before I shut the door, I notice a box with multi-colored hair sticking out of it—right away I remember the scary clown mask of my father's. He wears it to the local hall in Merville every Halloween.

I pull it out and study it. It's actually pretty evil-looking: a latex pasty face with long yellow teeth. Creepy.

My eyes catch the light coming from under the door of my parents' room, where Ivy will be sleeping for the next month. By the way the shadows are breaking through the light, I can tell she's just about to open the door. I quickly slide the mask over my head and stand with my back against the wall so she can't see me when she comes out.

I take a deep breath and wait as she walks out of the room. When she's a few steps past me, I growl loudly and grab her by the shoulders. Her body jumps as if a high bolt of electricity is running through it. When she quickly spins around and faces me, I scream in an evil voice. Terror causes her eyes to protrude and she opens her mouth to scream, but no noise comes out.

I start laughing and pull the mask off. Her expression morphs from terror to fury.

"I hate you, Paisley. There's something wrong with your head."

"It was a harmless Joke, Ivy," I say, still laughing. "Chill out."

She leans against the wall with her hand on her chest. "You could have given me a heart attack. Did you think of that?"

"Nope. Not even for a minute. You're twenty-seven, not eighty-seven. I was pretty sure you'd be ok."

Back in my room, I lie on my bed with a huge grin on my face. I know I should probably feel badly for scaring the crap out of her, but I don't. She's been a cruel bitch to me since I can remember, even on the rare occasions when I tried to offer my hand in friendship. Screw her. Who knows—maybe if I antagonize her enough, she'll go home, and I can work Ivy-free for the next month.

# Chapter Five

The alarm buzzes at 6 AM. Why the hell did I set it for so early?

Feeling sleepier than usual, I turn off the annoying sound, then roll onto my stomach and try to get back to sleep. No luck. Once I've been woken up, I'm up for the day.

I slowly get dressed and head down to the kitchen to make a quick cup of coffee and some toast before starting my day. As I eat, I peruse my list. I've got to tape over all of the light sockets and window frames in the cabins and put drop cloths on the floors so that Jasper can paint. Also, if there are any broken cupboard door hinges, I need to replace them. Somethings my father taught me well were how to use power tools and how to do basic maintenance—an important skill set when operating a summer cabin resort.

Ivy drifts through my mind. I try to imagine her using a drill and can't. She probably wouldn't even pick it up. Too worried about getting oil on her clothes.

After I finish eating, I walk to the maintenance shed and pick out the tools I'll need for the day. A multi-bit screwdriver kit, a hammer, and a few rolls of green painters' tape.

* * *

The first part of the day goes by quickly as I tape off the electrical outlets, doorknobs and windows. At noon I tackle the more arduous job of replacing hinges on the cupboards and the doors. As I work, my mind jumps between the present and the past. The first day I was brought to prison. The fear and the overwhelming feeling of having everything taken away from me. Then, I briefly imagine a small house in some secluded place, away from everyone—a peaceful and happy place.

A few more hours and about six slivers later, I decide that I've done enough for one day. My body isn't used to all of this manual labor. I feel physically bagged but somehow less burdened emotionally.

When I walk up to the main cabin, Ivy is just coming down the stairs. She tells me that she's running out to get dinner and she'll be back in an hour. I don't make eye contact, I just walk past her and into the house, shutting the door behind me.

As I kick off my shoes, I can't help but wonder what Miss Priss did all day while I was busting my ass. I bet she sat at my dad's desk and went on the computer, talking to her shallow friends. It makes me sick. Why didn't she get a list of physical jobs to do like I did?

Maybe her parents thought she'd break a nail and go into hysterics, who knows?

I grab a bag of Cheetos from the cupboard and flop down on the sofa, switching the TV on and mindlessly channel surfing. Before I know it, I'm drifting off to sleep.

I wake to the sight of Ivy standing over me. "I bought Chinese food. It's in the kitchen," she says, then walks away.

Even though I'd love to tell her where to stick her take-out food, my tummy is grumbling and my hunger is stronger than my will. When I get into the kitchen, the smell of the food makes my mouth water. Ivy passes me a combination meal in a container and a fork.

"Aren't you eating?" I ask.

"No. I ate while you were sleeping."

I carry my food to the table and sit down, cautiously looking over each of the three items in the container. What if she's still pissed over the clown mask incident? She was pretty terrified. What if she put something in my food like a laxative or a sleeping pill or something? I lift a pile of noodles with my fork and examine it. It looks fine. Then, I take a forkful of sweet and sour pork and smell it—nothing seems unusual. I look up at Ivy, who is standing with her arms folded and with a smile on her face. "Don't be stupid, Paisley. I'm not going to mess with your food."

I take a small nibble of the meal. It tastes fine, but maybe I'm just so hungry that I don't notice anything. Though, logically, she's probably telling me the truth. Why would she mess with my food and risk me getting sick? Her workload around here would double. I start to eat the tasty food, every couple of bites looking up at Ivy for a tell-tale sign of guilt— but she has a poker face.

Once I'm finished the entire dinner, I throw the container in the trash and rinse my fork. "Thanks," I say, heading for the door.

"Wait," she says. I turn to look at her, and I'm surprised by the look on her face. She looks slightly embarrassed. "I noticed how hard you worked today. Um…well, I guess I felt kind of bad, so I wanted to do something nice for you."

"Yeah, right."

"Really, Paisley." She looks me in the eyes. "I got to stay inside and do minimal chores while you worked in the cabins. So, I ran you a nice bath upstairs with candles and bubbles."

I stare at her, not believing what I'm hearing.

"Don't look so surprised, Paisley. You haven't seen me in a long time. I'm not the same girl I was when we were younger."

My first instinct is to call bullshit, but the sincere look on her face tells me that maybe, just maybe, she is telling the truth.

Not knowing what to say, I make my way up the stairs and into my room. Taking off all my clothes and grabbing a towel, I walk to the candlelit bathroom.

Sure enough, there's a tub full of water with lots of bubbles. The room is dim and the water inviting as I step slowly into the tub. The warm water soothes my tired, aching muscles—it feels great.

I can't believe she did this for me. Maybe she really has changed. It's a little hard to fathom, but I can't deny her efforts with getting me take-out food and now this—a candle-lit relaxing bubble bath.

After about twenty minutes, the temperature of the water drops and I decide to get out. I can hear movement coming from the wall behind me, my parents' room. An uncomfortable thought occurs to me. I should really thank Ivy.

I dry off quickly, blow out the fading tea-lights and walk out into the cold hallway, heading to Mom and Dad's room. I glance at myself in the small hallway mirror and I catch a glimpse of something on my neck. Getting closer to the mirror, I notice a dark smudge. I lick my finger and rub hard on the spot, but it doesn't fade. What the hell? Then, I slowly open my robe and look down at my naked body—I'm completely blue.

No way in hell.

"Ivy! What did you do?" I scream.

I hear a loud cackle coming from behind the bedroom door. I want to bust my way into my parents' room and strangle her, but I know that the longer I let this color sink into my skin, the harder it will be to get off. I rush back to my bathroom, turn on the light and stare down at the indigo water that's in the tub. "You're so dead, Ivy."

I quickly empty the water from the tub, grab a bar of soap from the sink and turn on the shower. I scrub relentlessly and still, my body is the same color it was—navy blue. Sonofabitch! I have no idea how to get this crap off. I shut off the shower and smother shampoo all over me, then sit down and wait on the side of the tub. Maybe letting the soap sink into my skin for a while will get some of this dye off. As I wait, my mind explores revenge scenarios. Filling her car with stinky wet kelp and other slimy beach finds, or putting Krazy Glue in her lip-gloss.

I can't believe I fell for her nice-girl routine. *"I've changed,"* she said. What a bunch of crap. She's changed alright, for the worse.

A half hour later and I'm starting to shiver. I stand up and slowly wash off the shampoo, hoping my skin will be back to normal once the suds wash off. Thankfully, I see the shampoo foam turning a light blue as I rub and rinse my skin. By the time I'm finished, my legs and arms are sore from all of the friction. Once I'm dried off with my once-white, now blue towel, I examine my body. It's lighter. Though I'm still sporting a blue tinge, it's not half as dark as it was.

I'm sure after a dozen or so shampoo soaks, I'll be back to normal. In the meantime, I'm dedicating all of my concentration on how to get that idiot back for this.

* * *

The next two days are high-tension around the house. I've been lurking around, wondering what Princess Nightmare is going to do to me next. She's just as paranoid —I can tell by the way she waits until I'm downstairs before she leaves her room.

On a positive note, I've been working like a dog in the cabins, quickly accomplishing every item on the list that my dad left. In some ways, I wonder if I'm working so hard because I'm still wanting his approval—pointless.

While I'm working in a cabin, I look up and notice Ivy leaving in her car. I smile. *This is the perfect time.* I put down the roll of tape and head over to the main house. Courtenay is the closest town, so no matter how fast she is at whatever she's doing, she won't be back for at least an hour. I'm motivated by vengeance because though I've managed to scrub my body hue down to a light turquoise, the horror of seeing my blue skin in the mirror that evening is fresh in my mind.

I guess a more mature and grounded person would let it slide to avoid conflict. Not this girl. The last thing I'll do is let her think that she's won.

I walk into my parents' room and look for something of Ivy's. The room is in the exact same order as my dad left it. Wow, she's a clean freak—another annoying characteristic. When I open the closet, I see the big suitcase she brought in the day my parents left. Then I look up and notice that all of her clothes are hanging neatly in color-coded order—how nauseating.

I pull her suitcase out of the closet and put it on the bed. When I unzip it, I see little clear bags with labels on them, *Underwear*, *Bras* and *Socks*. Seriously? This chick needs to lighten the hell up. As I stare down into the case, nothing obvious jumps out at me as a great revenge idea. I casually look around the room. There's a computer, a stapler and a jar with pens and a pair of scissors in it. Hmmm, scissors. I get up, grab the implement of destruction and sit on the bed.

I open each little package and dump all of the under garments and socks onto the bed. Next, I grab a red lace bra and cut a chunk out of the front of the cups. Then, I repeat the same steps to two other bras before setting my sights on her socks. Methodically, I snip off the toe of every pair. When I'm finished, I gently fold the items and stuff them back in their labelled bags. I place the suitcase exactly as I found it in the bottom of the closet and collect the fabric bits before heading downstairs. After I grab a saucer from the kitchen and a camping lighter from the front room cabinet, I pile the fabric pieces on the dish, sit on the couch, and wait.

After waiting for a good hour, boredom sets in and I decide to go back to work. Hopefully, when Ivy shows up, I can get to the house before she does.

Every few minutes I see Jasper as he brings pails of paint and brushes inside cabins. Usually, he waits until nobody is around before he starts his work, probably to avoid the possibility of interaction. The guy has been here forever and I can almost count the times I've spoken to him. Like my mother always says, 'He's a true hermit.'

As soon as I finish prepping the last cabin, I see the little black convertible pull up. I quickly drop whatever is in my hand and head toward the main house. I walk quietly across the lot so she doesn't notice me. As soon as she goes into the back seat and starts loading herself with bags, I move quickly up the front stairs and into the house.

I sit on the sofa, grab the lighter and light each piece of fabric on the saucer. A minute or two later, Ivy staggers through the door. "I saw you sneaking in, Paisley. You could've helped me with the groceries. They're not just for me, you know!"

"Wow. Yeah, that's quite an armload you've got there. I had no idea it was groceries, I just assumed you bought more of that stinky perfume and makeup refills."

"Very funny, you jerk. What are you burning?" she asks as she makes her way behind me and into the kitchen.

I smile and say nothing.

I hear her set the groceries down before walking back into the front room. "Are you at least going to help me put the food away?"

"Sure, as soon as you help me with all of the cabin prepping."

"Whatever, Paisley. We both have our own lists to do. And put whatever it is you're burning out—it's starting to stink." She peers over the sofa at the saucer. "What is all of that, anyway?" She stares at my mini pile of burning fabric. "Where did you find pink and red lace, and why are you…"

She pauses. Her eyes grow wide. "No. No. No!" she yells, turning and running up the stairs. I grin, put out the burning lace and head back outside. Feeling vindicated, I walk across the lot with an almost swagger to my gait. I'm just in front of a rental cabin when I hear Ivy screaming from behind.

I turn just in time to see her jumping down the front stairs and heading toward me. Whatever she plans on yelling at me, I'm just going to laugh—touché, Ivy. You got what was coming to you.

Though, as she runs toward me, red-faced and livid, it occurs to me that her objective isn't to throw insults. I quickly stand up straight and push my shoulders back, making myself appear bigger, more intimidating, like what you're supposed to do if you see a bear in the wild. But she just keeps coming, showing no signs of slowing down. When she reaches me, I open my mouth to speak, but before I can say anything, I feel a hard slap to the side of my face. Before I have time to react, she grabs a handful of my hair and yanks down.

"Let go of my hair!" I scream.

"You ruined my clothes. I'm going to kick the shit out of you."

"You're lucky that's all I did, after you dyed my skin blue!"

As she continues to pull on my hair, I reach up and grab a handful of hers, tugging hard until she screams. Pretty soon we're locked in a violent huddle, rolling around in the dirt, neither of us willing to give up. Then, after what seems like forever, I feel a leathery hand grab the back of my neck and squeeze tightly.

"Let go!" Jasper says in a deep, angry voice.

Immediately my hand opens, releasing my grip on Ivy's hair.

"Ivy, you let go, too!" he orders.

She lets go of me and we both roll onto our backs, panting as we look up at the very upset Jasper.

"You two are behaving like a couple of children. Get your shit together and grow up or I'm calling your parents and telling them to come home early," he says, before turning and walking away.

"I can't believe he actually spoke to us," I say, still trying to catch my breath.

"Me either," Ivy says.

We turn and look at each other, both covered in dirt and looking like we've just been pulled through a knothole backward.

"Whatever shampoo you use makes your hair pretty soft," I say.

Both of us burst into laughter.

After we compose ourselves, we get up and brush off the dirt.

"Do you want a cup of coffee?" Ivy asks.

"It depends. Are you going to burn it?"

She makes a face, which dissolves into a smile. "Where's your sense of adventure?"

Exhausted, we both walk back to the house. I'm glad my father wasn't here to witness what just happened. I can only hope that Jasper doesn't decide to tell. Dad would probably call my parole officer and all hell would break loose.

* * *

For whatever reason, Ivy and I spend the next few days cohabitating with civility. We eat dinner together in front of the TV, share the house chores like vacuuming and doing the dishes—she even helps me prep the cabins. I guess everything needed to come to a head and explode between us before we could find a peaceful medium.

Not surprisingly, we haven't seen Jasper since he broke up our fight. I've never seen Jasper pissed off before, and that was definitely the first time he's ever laid a hand on me. Impressively strong for an old codger.

* * *

My thumb flicks over the back cover while I read the last page of *The Great Gatsby*, a good book with a clear message about watching what you wish for—I get it!

Feeling a bit restless, I walk over to the window and stare out into the evening. The leaves on nearby trees are still, meaning there's little wind. When I look up, I see that the sky is clear. A perfect summer's night to be on the beach.

When I walk upstairs to get a sweater, I hear Ivy tapping away on the computer. I get a sudden urge to invite her to the beach, but even though we seem to have found a peaceful understanding between us, I'm nervous to ask. I hesitate at the top of the stairs, then go to my room for the sweater.

Back in the hallway, as I slide my hoodie over my head, Ivy's door opens and she walks out.

"Hey," she says, nodding.

I nod back. "I'm just getting ready to go to the beach. It's a beautiful night—I don't want to waste it by sitting inside. I thought maybe I'd light a small fire."

"Great idea." She pauses. "Do you mind if I come along?"

"Sure." I shrug, acting indifferent, but I am secretly happy that she asked.

She tells me that she has to finish something on the computer, but she'll walk down to the beach after she's done.

\* \* \*

The warm sea air greets me as I step off the wooden porch and onto the gravel, and I hear the rushing sound of waves. I pull my shoes off so I can walk the trail to the beach barefoot.

Once at the long, sandy shore, I place my shoes beside a log and then make my way to the water's edge, letting the waves crawl up my feet as I look across the water at the silhouette of Savary Island. As I slowly inhale the sea air and take in my surroundings, a sense of contentment and peace comes over me.

After a few moments, I decide to look for some dry pieces of beach wood so I can start the fire. I gather a small armload of wood from the dry ground and set them in a pile on the beach. After I crumple a few pages of newspaper into a ball, then arrange small pieces of wood on top, I light the edge of the paper and sit back. Just as the smallest pieces of kindling start to light, I see Ivy walking up the beach toward me, wearing shorts and a sweatshirt and carrying a plastic bag.

"Hey, you've already got the wood lit. That was fast!" She sits down on the other side of the small fire.

"What did you bring with you, a fire extinguisher?"

"Why, are we going to need one?"

"I bloody well hope not."

"We should be ok, as long as neither one of us tries to cook."  From the bag she pulls a bottle of wine and two glasses. "I thought maybe we could indulge a little." She smiles.

"I'll have some. Just don't tell my parole officer…or my father." I wink.

I get up, walk over and sit down beside her, holding the glasses while she pours the red wine.

"Y'know, if we were still enemies, there's no way I would be drinking this. I'd probably end up with green teeth."

"Yeah, sorry about dying your skin blue."

"It's alright. To be honest, a part of me was impressed that you came up with it. A very small part of me."

When our drinks are poured, I hand Ivy a glass. She takes it and balances it on the sand before lying back, looking up at the dark sky. "I love the stars. I could stay out here all night and watch them."

The fire crackles as it eats its way through the pieces of kindling. I quickly grab bigger bits of wood and place them over the flames. Taking a sip of wine, I look at Ivy, her toned bare legs glowing from the yellow of the fire. She's flawless, there's no debating that. I was always so angry with Ivy that I never really let myself admire her. Her soft blond hair is strewn messily over the sand and her lips are tinted a subtle red from the wine, making them look full and inviting. When she moves her foot suddenly, I quickly turn my head away.

"You should see these stars, Paisley. They're extra bright tonight."

I glance at the fire and make sure it's burning well before setting my glass in the sand and lying down, my arm a few inches from hers.

"Do you see the Big Dipper?" she asks, pointing upward.

"I do. You're right, the stars do seem brighter tonight."

For the next little while, we say nothing. We just lie still, letting our eyes dance from star to star. The cadence from the waves emits an almost musical accompaniment to the dreamlike mood. Then, completely unexpectedly, I feel her hand touch mine.

"Oh, sorry," she says. "Wrong side. I was feeling for my glass."

I smile without looking at her.

She rolls onto her side with her drink in hand and looks at me. "Can I ask you something personal?"

"Uh oh. Should I be nervous?"

"Did you love her?"

"Did I love who?"

"C'mon, Paisley. You know who I'm talking about." She nudges me.

"Ah yes, Storm." I sigh, feeling a dull ache in my chest. "I don't know. I thought I did. She was different, so wild and fearless. I guess she made me feel alive."

"So, it was more of a crush or a lust thing then?"

"I don't know, Ivy. Either way, it doesn't matter now. A lot has happened since then."

"I know. I'm sorry that you had to go through that hell. I don't think I could've survived if it were me."

"You'd be surprised what you can endure if you have to."

"Do you feel bitter toward her now?"

"No. To tell you the truth, I try not to think of her at all."

Ivy nods. "I heard that you wouldn't rat her out to the cops. I respected you for that. But there must have been times you questioned your decision. I mean, it must've been unbearable in there."

"It wasn't all bad, but definitely not a place I'd book a vacation."

Ivy smiles, then asks, "What was the worst part about it?"

It doesn't take me long to come out with the name. "Violet."

"Who's that?"

"She was this horrid chick that kind of ran the cell block I was in."

"What made her horrid?"

"The lack of a soul." I shrug. "She picked on everyone. She would beat the shit out of you for looking at her and then beat the shit out of you for not looking at her. She was unpredictable."

"You had to contend with her for the whole nine months you were in?"

I tell Ivy about how Violet used to randomly beat on me, until she found out that I knew Storm. After that, Violet was tolerant of me.

"She quit beating you just because you knew Storm? Why?"

"I don't really know. I did hear from another girl that Storm and Violet were once an item. But I have no real proof of that, and honestly, I don't really care." I dig my fingers in the sand. "I'm out, and I want to do everything I can to forget about the last nine months."

"That's a great idea," she says, lying down and looking up to the stars. "You have a clean start, Paisley. You're free and you can do whatever you want now."

I grin. "Like going swimming in the sea in the middle of the night?"

She turns her head to me and smiles. "What? Have you lost it?"

"Well, *you* don't have to do it. I mean...if you're scared?"

"Scared? What does that word mean?" She sits up.

I stand and brush off my sweats. *Oh no, I'm wearing sweats. I totally forgot. How am I supposed to swim in these? Me and my big mouth.*

Ivy pulls off her sweatshirt, revealing a tight white tank top. Then, she looks down at my pants. "Interesting swimwear. I'm not sure how effective that will be in the water, though."

Since I've already said it, I've got to go through with it. I tell Ivy to turn around, then I slide off my sweatpants. Next, I take off my hoodie and drop it on the sand. She's still turned away from me when I run past her toward the water. "Let's do this."

Ivy laughs as she runs to catch up.

When I first feel the water touch my bare legs, it's cold—really cold—but after wading in up to my waist, I start to get used to it. I turn and see Ivy slowly enter the water with her arms held close to her body. "Wow! Chilly, huh?"

"I'm telling myself it's refreshing."

She walks up beside me and shivers.

"You know, Ivy, there's one way to warm up quickly."

"What's that?" she says, clenching her teeth.

I slide my hand into the water and lightly splash her. Laughing, she arches her back and tries to get away.

"Wait, Ivy. Come back. If you get splashed, the wind hits you and you get cold. All you have to do is dunk down into the water to feel warmer."

She looks at me. "Makes sense to me," she says, before putting both of her hands in the water and then power drenching me. Before I know it, we're in a water war, giggling and squealing. Once we've tired out, we swim out a ways and tread water as we look up at the starry sky, which is an endless dome over us. I can't remember when I've felt this free.

Then, Ivy shrieks and swears that she felt something big brush up against her leg. I try and keep her calm as we swim back to shore, but the truth is, I'm kind of creeped out now, too. I've been a water baby my whole life, so not much scares me about swimming in the sea. Still, with how dark it is out here, my imagination is starting to get away with me—words like sea lion, orca and white shark run through my mind.

As soon as we are close enough to shore that our feet touch the sand, we slow our pace and walk the rest of the way out. By the time we reach our stuff, the flames have died down to embers. I quickly get dressed and use the wine glasses to get water and soak the coals before gathering our things. As we walk to the house, I can't deny that I'm feeling attracted to Ivy. Something tells me that I always have been.

# Chapter Six

After our amazing evening on the beach, the next few days are cloudy and wet. It doesn't matter what the season, rain in the Pacific Northwest isn't only predictable, it's expected. As my father always says, we don't tan here, we rust.

As soon as the weather clears up, Ivy convinces me to go running with her in the mornings before we start our day. As much as I'm not much into jogging, I seize the opportunity to spend more time with Ivy. Today she's mapped out a grueling five-mile trek, starting at the resort then down the old Island Highway before turning around and jogging all the way home. Everything in me wants to fake a pulled leg muscle so I can sit around and watch TV until she gets back, but I don't want her to think I'm lazy and out of shape.

After we have a light breakfast of fruit and granola, we get dressed and head out. Thankfully, Ivy isn't jogging too fast. I think she senses that I'm nowhere near as agile or as energetic as she is. We slowly jog for a while before we get to the old Island Highway. Since traffic is scarce, we're able to jog side by side. After about five minutes of being on the old highway, a doe and her fawn jump out of the woods and onto the road in front of us. We quickly stop and watch as the mother deer waits patiently for her baby.

"They're so beautiful," Ivy says.

I glance at her as she watches the deer. She smiles as the morning sun shines on her porcelain skin, making it glow. She looks so beautiful. Not to mention, I love how much she's infatuated with the animals, just another attribute of her character that I'm attracted to.

When the deer pass by and we resume our run, we're only on the road for about twenty minutes before clouds form overhead and it starts to rain. Thankfully, our outing is cut short and we are forced to head home. Of course, I curse the weather and do my best to sound disappointed.

For the rest of the day, I work in the cabins while Ivy stays in the office, answering phones and working on the computer. When the sun goes down, we're both tired, so we microwave a couple of bowls of soup, sit on the sofa and watch an old black and white movie. Slowly, we inch closer together until we're side by side. After the movie, we give each other a quick hug and then head to our own rooms. Once I'm nestled on my bed, a feeling of contentment comes over me. I think about Ivy and smile before drifting off to sleep.

* * *

I wake to a cool breeze flowing over my body and the sound of the shutters clacking against the open windowsill. I look over at the alarm, the red digital letters glowing in the darkness. I grab my sheet and wrap it tightly around me.

The noise coming from the shutters gets louder and louder, until I can't take it anymore. I push off the covers and slowly sit up. Sliding off the bed, my feet touch the surprisingly cold floor. It's summer—no matter if it's nighttime or not, there's no way it should be this cold in my room.

I quickly walk to the open window and pull down on the frame to close it, but no matter how hard I try, it won't shut. I'm starting to shake so badly that my fingers are aching, making it hard to move them. I grab onto the window frame again, this time tighter. I decide to use my body weight when I pull down, hopefully unjamming the window. I give a strong heave, using all of my energy. The window unsticks, comes sliding down and crashes into the sill. A glass pane explodes and lands in shards all around my feet.

Scared of getting cut, I gently slide one of my feet toward the door so I can turn on the light. As soon as I slide my other foot, I feel a spike of glass slice into me. I open my mouth to scream but no noise comes out. My body is so cold that my lungs are restricted. With no choice, I keep walking. Every couple of steps, more glass pierces my skin. The pain in my feet intensifies and the only thing I can see is the small puffs of white breath coming out of my mouth.

Then, I hear a noise coming from outside the door: "Ivy?" I yell, but it comes out as a whisper.

I hear the doorknob squeak as it slowly turns. *Thank God, she's heard me and she's coming in to help.* I stop walking and stand still in the middle of the room. Slowly, the door opens, casting light on the floor. I look down and see thousands of pieces of jagged, sparkling glass—an unbelievable amount, considering how small the windowpane was. I look back at the door. The light from the hallway is silhouetting the figure in the doorway. Only, the shadow doesn't match Ivy's body at all. This person is big like a man, with broad shoulders and long thick legs.

"Who's there?" I ask, my voice quiet and shaky.

Suddenly, the light flicks on, temporarily blinding me. I quickly rub my eyes and strain to focus. Standing in the doorway is my father. His brows are furrowed, and his mouth is tightly pursed. "What have you done?" he says, scanning the strewn glass on the floor. His voice booms.

*Why is he here and not in Florida? Where's Mom?* I want to ask him but I'm afraid to.

"It was an accident," I say, suddenly finding my voice.

"Look at the mess you've made."

"I'm sorry. I'll clean it up, I promise." Tears run down my cheeks as I look down and notice two large pools of blood around each of my feet. I start to feel woozy. "I'm cut pretty badly, Dad. Please, will you help me?"

"It's always something with you, isn't it?"

"I'm sorry Dad. Please, just help me get out of this glass and I'll fix—"

"Bullshit you'll fix it. You're nothing but a useless piece of trash."

"Why are you saying that?" I sob, feeling empty.

"Do you know what I think? I think you purposely screwed up your life to get revenge on me."

"Why would I want to do that?"

"Because I don't love you."

"Dad!" The tears are flowing so heavily that I can barely see him anymore. "Please don't say that. I love you very much. I'm so sorry that I disappointed you. All I've ever wanted was for you to accept me as I am."

At first, I hear a subtle chuckle but soon it turns into an evil and almost maniacal fit of laughter. "I don't accept you. You disgust me."

A throbbing pain grows in my heart and I drop my head. As I cry, huge tears fall from my chin and land in the puddles of blood at my feet.

"It's time you pay for the things you've done," he says, before turning off the light and slamming the door.

I sprint forward, picking up more glass in the bottoms of my feet. When I reach the door, I grab the handle and turn and pull but it won't budge. Out of desperation, I bang on the wood with the palms of my hands. "Daddy, don't leave me here. I'm sorry. Come back. Please come back."

I slide my hand over the wall to the light switch, but when I try to flick the light on, the room stays dark.

"Please. Please come back. I'll change. I'll be good. I promise." My sobs are so heavy that my body weakens and I slide down the door.

"I love you Dad, please come back for me," I whisper. I feel hollow, like nothing. I just want the pain in my chest to stop. I want to fade away.

\* \* \*

"Paisley. You're ok. I'm here."

I gasp when the warm hand touches my shoulder. My eyes spring open. Ivy is sitting in front of me on my bed and I'm lying on my side with my head on the pillow.

"Ivy, you got the door open. I need to get help. I'm cut really badly." I sit up.

"Where?" she says, looking worried.

"My feet," I say, pulling the sheet off.

When I look down, I see my two feet, clean and uninjured. Disoriented, I put my hands over my wet face.

"Where are you injured, Paisley?" Ivy says, looking at my legs.

"I...I don't know. I thought I had cut my feet on the glass." I uncover my face and look over to the window—which is completely intact.

"Paisley, I heard you calling out in your sleep, so I came in. You were just having a bad dream."

I look at her. "It was so real, Ivy. My dad was here." I lay my head back down on the pillow. Tears form again in my eyes.

"Our parents are still in Florida. It's just you and me here." She gently rubs my shoulder.

"He was a monster, Ivy. He was so cold. I had cut my feet from the broken window and he wouldn't help me, he just said things."

"What things?"

"How I'm a disappointment to him. How he doesn't love me." I hide my face in the pillow so she can't see me cry.

Ivy slides her body onto the bed and moves against me. She wraps her arm around my shoulder and rests her head next to mine." It's not true, Paisley."

"What isn't?" I ask, my voice muffled inside the pillow.

"It's not true that your dad doesn't love you."

"You don't know, Ivy. He can't even stand to look at me. He hates me."

"He doesn't hate you, sweetie. I don't know if your mom told you this, but when you were

82

away, in jail, he would talk about you all the time."

I move my face away from the pillow and look at her, our faces only inches apart. "What do you mean?"

"Well, for starters, when someone brings up fishing, your dad talks about when you and he would go out on the water for hours. How you always made a great day out of it, regardless if there were any fish caught or not. Also, whenever my dad or yours would discuss doing cabin renos, your father would mention how you and he would figure out the best way to do things, together. He was always reminiscing about the time you spent together."

"If that's true, then why is he so cold to me now? A huge space formed between us as soon as he found out I was gay. Ever since then, we've been like oil and water."

"I think his problem is less to do with you being gay and more that he's worried you're taking a difficult path. And when you ended up in jail because of a gay lover, he was scared for you. He felt helpless." She shrugs. "I could be wrong, but I think when you got out of prison, he was afraid to reach out to you, afraid that something else bad would happen to you. To protect himself, he pulled away."

I sniff and wipe my moist eyes. "You were a lot easier to figure out when I thought you were dumb."

We laugh and she hugs me tightly.

"You have to let yourself unravel a bit, Paisley. It's the only way you're going to work things out. You've been through hell."

I nod and smile. "I guess you're right."

"Are you feeling a little better now?"

"Yeah, I think so. Thanks for coming to my rescue."

"Anytime." She smiles, sitting up.

I reach out and put my hand on her arm. "Ivy?"

"Yeah?"

"Will you stay with me tonight? I don't want to be alone."

She smiles, then snuggles in next to me.

"You don't snore, do you?" I say, squeezing her waist.

"I'm not sure. If I were you, I'd fall asleep first, just in case."

"Thanks again for being here," I say, pulling the sheet over us.

\* \* \*



\* \* \*


Silently I lie next to her, watching as the morning sun gently sweeps across her face, giving her an ethereal glow. She's beautiful in this natural state, her mouth slightly open and her hair disheveled and strewn over the pillow. Then a racket of squawking gulls passes by the window, causing her eyelashes to flicker. Slowly she opens her eyes fully and sees me gazing at her and smiling.

"Good morning," I say softly.

She smiles back. "No more bad dreams?"

"No."

"I'm glad. So, you slept ok?"

"Not really."

"Why not?"

"Well, it turns out that you do snore, and loudly, too. You kept me up all night."

Embarrassed, she looks down. "I'm sorry."

She looks so remorseful, I can't keep up the lie. "Just kidding, you slept as quietly as a mouse."

"You're a jerk," she says, laughing and using her pillow to hit me.

I tickle her. She tickles me back and then climbs on top of me, using her legs to pin my arms down. With my knees up, I use my stomach muscles to try and bump her off me, but I lose my strength.

"You're in so much trouble when I get up."

"Really? I don't know, girl. Seems I've got you in a pretty compromising situation. I don't think I'm too worried."

"I'm letting you do this to me."

We giggle.

"I can do whatever I want," she says, "and there's not much you can do about it."

"What do you mean by that?" I say, squirming, but not really wanting to get away.

85

"Like, I can do this," she says, gently grabbing the front of my bra and releasing it.

"I see. And what else could you do to me?"

She smiles then leans down, her golden hair tickling my cheeks. When she gets close enough, I can feel the warmth of her breath on me. "This," she whispers before pressing her soft lips against mine.

An electric shiver runs over me, and I instantly feel goosebumps form on my skin. I can feel her body shake as she kisses me—I'm shaking too.

After a long moment, she sits up and looks at me, her face a shade of rose. She closes her eyes, opens them and says, "That was intense."

"I know. I felt it too."

She's embarrassed. "Do you want to go downstairs for breakfast? I'm starving."

I nod.

She gets off me and walks out of the room. I roll over onto my side and smile. She could be what I've been looking for my whole life, but because of who we are, I've never considered her—until now. I get out of bed, stretch and head down to the kitchen.

* * *

"Do you know if we have any cold cereal?" she says, reaching up and opening cupboards.

"I think I ate the last of it a couple of days ago."

"No problem. I bought some eggs the other day. We'll just make French toast. We should be able to master that."

"You're giving us a lot of credit."

Ivy gets out my mother's recipe book while I make coffee. "So, what did you eat while living in the city?" she asks suddenly.

"For breakfast, mostly fruit. For lunch, anything that was microwavable and for dinner, whatever was the special at one of the local take-out places. Sometimes I would get really adventurous and make a salad."

Ivy smiles. "I guess we're pretty pathetic, huh?"

We laugh.

When the coffee is finished, I pour Ivy a mug and then help her with the recipe. I accidently crack the eggs too hard and spend a few minutes fishing out shell fragments with a fork. Ivy gets a frying pan out of the cupboard and puts it on the element while I whisk the eggs.

"Ok, now we just need bread," she says, looking around the kitchen.

"Did you buy any?"

"I don't think I did," she says apologetically.

"Ok. Well, I think if we add a bit of milk to the eggs, we should be able to make an omelet."

I ask her to check the fridge for cheese and after mixing the egg and milk together, I empty the bowl into the pan and turn the dial to medium heat.

Ivy slices some cheese, in my opinion, a little thicker than we need, but I don't say anything. She lays the little cheese slabs over the raw egg then we grab our coffees and sit at the table and wait.

"So, what should we do today?" she asks.

"I don't know. I think there's some calking that needs doing in a couple of the rentals."

"No. I don't mean work. I mean we should do something fun."

I smile. "I guess it wouldn't hurt to take a day off."

"Good. So, what should we do?"

"I don't know. What if we take a drive up to Nymph Falls? I've been thinking about going there since I got back. Maybe we can stop at a deli and then walk on the trails?"

"That's a great idea."

I start to smell something unfriendly coming from the pan. I quickly get up and walk to the stove. Inside the pan is a burnt-edged yellow blob that is raw in the middle. The cheese hunks aren't even close to melting.

"How does it look?" she asks.

"Well, it doesn't look like much yet. I think we should fold it in half now, to melt the cheese."

Ivy joins me at the stove, holding a spatula. I get out of the way while she pushes the flipper under the egg, lifts it up and half-manages to fold it over. The whole bottom of the omelet is burnt.

"Yummy, half raw, half burned breakfast," she says, staring down into the pan.

"Is it really possible that we can both be this inadequate in the kitchen? I mean, seriously."

We look at each other and burst into laughter.

"No wonder we are both gay, can you imagine if we were each traditionally married and had children?"

"We'd have the skinniest families on the West Coast," I say, still laughing.

She turns the stove off. "So, I'm thinking that our best bet is to pick something up on the way to the falls. Are you down with that?"

"Big time," I agree.

We go upstairs and get ready for our adventure. Because the forecast is calling for a sunny day, I've opted to wear shorts and a tank top. Just as I'm brushing my teeth, Ivy walks in, wearing jean shorts and a t-shirt. She wraps her arms around my waist from behind as I finish brushing. I feel good, the best I've felt in a very long time. She tells me that she's going downstairs to clean up the debris from our breakfast attempt while I finish getting ready.

I'm halfway down the stairs, pulling my hair into a loose pony, when I hear the house phone ring in the living room. I hear Ivy greet the caller with the usual spiel: "Good morning, Stogan's Resort. How may I help you?"

I walk up behind her while she has the receiver to her ear and teasingly pinch her bum, she turns to me and smiles. Then, I lean against the back of the sofa, waiting for her to get off the phone so we can leave.

Suddenly, her face loses its usual rosy glow. She looks shocked. Without saying another word to the caller, she holds the phone toward me. "It's for you."

"Me?" I say. Who would be calling me? Nobody even knows I'm here, except the parole officer.

When I take the phone from her, she crosses her arms and then walks up the stairs. Confused, I put my ear to the receiver. "Hello?"

"Paisley? Is this really you?"

As soon as I hear the voice, my brain freezes, and I can't speak.

"Paisley, it's me." Her voice is excited.

Composing myself, I say, "I know who this is. How did you get this number?"

"That's all you're thinking about? How I got the number? You're not happy to hear from me?"

"How did you get this number, Storm?" I repeat bluntly.

"Violet told me where you were. I guess your cell mate told her and then she told me. Why? Is it bad that I'm calling?"

"What do you think, Storm? You put me through hell. Did you really think I'd be overjoyed to hear from you?"

"I know how you must be feeling, Paisley, and I don't blame you. I'd hate me too if I were you. That's why I'm calling. I really want to explain things to you. I think you deserve that much."

"So, say your piece then."

"I want to, but not on the phone. I really need to talk to you in person. For the last nine months, I've been tortured by the guilt of you going to jail because of something I did. I really want to see you face-to-face so I can properly explain."

"I don't want to see you, Storm. I just want to be left alone."

"It doesn't sound like you're alone."

"Ivy, the co-owner's daughter, is the one that answered the phone. Other than that, I'm alone." I immediately feel regret for sharing that information with her. I don't want her to know anything about my life now.

"I know you're upset, Paisley. But can't you just take like ten minutes to quickly speak with me? I don't have long to talk right now because I have to leave to go back to Vancouver."

"What do you mean by *back* to Vancouver? Where are you now?"

"I've been in Victoria for a couple of months. As soon as I got back from Mexico, I came here and stayed with friends. I've really gotten my shit together, Paisley. It's been really hard, but I finally feel like I can do something good with my life."

"Yeah, right. You'll have to excuse my apprehension."

She sighs. "I deserved that."

"I have to go now, Storm. I've got things to do."

"I understand. Could I stop by in a couple of days so I can quickly speak with you?"

"I don't think it's a good idea. There's no reason for you to tell me whatever it is you feel you have to say. It's over now."

"I see," she says in a somber tone.

"Goodbye, Storm. I hope you have a good life." I hang up.

* * *

When I get upstairs, Ivy is sitting at the desk, the glow from the computer monitor reflecting on her face.

I walk up behind the chair and put my hands on her shoulders. She tenses and moves away.

"What's the matter?"

"Nothing. I just remembered that I have work to do. I'm trying to concentrate."

"What about our day at the falls?"

"Yeah, you know what? I don't think that's such a great idea, Paisley."

"You were all happy about going until the phone rang. Is that why you're acting this way? Because of the phone call?"

She turns to me, her face cold. "I couldn't care less who calls you or doesn't call you, Paisley. But what I do care about is finishing this work, so could I please have some privacy?"

At first, I'm taken aback and not sure what to say. Then, I try to reason with her. "Ivy, Storm called. I told her that I didn't want anything to do with her and then I hung up. That was it."

"That's fascinating, Paisley. I wonder how she got your number?"

"Crazy Violet from jail gave it to her. She didn't get it from me, if that's what you're implying." I'm starting to feel a bit defensive.

"Paisley, I don't care. Now will you please leave me alone?"

I can tell by the tone of her voice that she's serious. Any more attempts at working things out right now would be futile and would probably end in an argument. I don't want that, especially considering how close we've become.

I slowly walk out of the bedroom and close the door. As I walk downstairs, I feel confused at Storm's unexpected call, and upset that there seems to be a divide between Ivy and me now.

* * *

With our great plans for the day now obliterated, I decide to work on the cabins to occupy my time. It's going to be a long day of feeling like crap over Ivy. It figures. Just when things were going so well.

I get so wrapped up in what I'm doing that I lose track of time. When I finally look up at the clock in the cabin, it's 3PM. I've been going for hours without food, water or a break.

On my way back to the main house I see Ivy sitting on the porch with a book in her hand. Excitement comes over me but is soon replaced with sadness. Have we lost our closeness? Will she ever look at me again the way she did before she kissed me in bed this morning?

Not knowing what to say to her, I cross the lot and walk down to the shore. I'll hang out down here for a while and hopefully she leaves the porch, so I don't have to face her. I walk over to a log and I'm just about to sit down when I hear someone yelling in the distance—a male voice. Quickly, I walk to the water's edge and look in both directions. I hear the voice again, this time it's louder. Maybe it's someone calling for their dog over on Savary Island? Sound travels across water—even if the person is miles away, they sound like they're right in front of you.

I wait a couple of minutes and when I don't hear anything, I decide to go back to the log. Just as I'm turning around to face the beach, I catch a glimpse of something yellow coming around the point. I immediately identify the object as a kayak and there's a silhouette of a person sitting in it.

"Hey, is everything ok?" I yell.

The figure waves his arms in my direction. "I've lost my paddle and it's too far for me to swim to shore," he hollers back. I can tell that this is an older male by the croakiness of his voice. At first, I consider calling for help, but my phone is in the house and by the time I go to get it, the small vessel would be carried away by the current. The only logical option I have, to ensure the man's safety, is to swim out and pull the kayak to shore.

I look down at what I'm wearing—khaki work pants with lots of pockets to put tape and paintbrushes in and a long, baggy t-shirt. Seeing no choice, I peel off my clothes until I'm standing in my sports bra and underwear, then quickly wade into the water. When I'm waist deep, I dive in and swim with strong strokes toward the man.

The farther I get from shore, the more I feel the current fighting against me. I look up and see the man leaning to one side of the Kayak and doing his best to paddle with one hand in my direction. By the time I finally reach him, I'm out of breath and my legs are aching. The man looks to be in his seventies, with age spots on his arms and a sunken, worried look on his face.

"Are you ok?" I ask, trying to catch my breath.

"Yes. Fine, thank you."

"What happened?"

"I'm staying at a cabin in the next bay over. I rented one of their kayaks and headed into the cove. I noticed I was going too far out but when I tried to turn around, I dug the oar too far into the water and it got away from me." He looks embarrassed.

"It happens. Don't worry, I'll get you to shore, just relax."

"Thanks, Miss."

"It's Paisley."

"Pleased to meet you, Paisley. I'm Stanley."

I grab the rope on the front of the watercraft and start heading to shore when I see Ivy standing on the beach looking our way. "Are you ok out there?" she yells.

"Great," I answer, secretly pleased she's witnessing my heroic rescue.

"Thanks again, Paisley," Stanley says. "I feel the fool for getting myself into this jam to begin with."

"Trust me, Stanley. There are far worse jams to get yourself into," I say, with some authority on the subject.

Then, I hear Ivy holler from the beach. I turn and see that she's jumping up and down and pointing behind us. Oh great. Now what?

I turn and look in the direction she's motioning. Just then, I hear a loud blast of what sounds like compressed air being released. Stanley gasps, then shouts, "Look! Orca. They're right here!"

My first thoughts are, big mammal, big teeth, and how far I am from shore. I can't get in the kayak, it's too small—I'd more than likely overturn the small boat and send old Stanley into the chuck. I take a deep breath and try to stay calm as I slowly breaststroke toward the beach.

"Look at their huge dorsal fins," exclaims Stanley.

*Keep it to yourself old man, because if I get any more terrified, I'm pretty sure I'll be running across the water and stranding your Orca-happy ass out here alone.*

As I head to shore, I try to ignore the images of killer whale teeth that are flashing through my mind. *KILLER whale, not gentle and sweet whale, but KILLER whale. Technically, they're not even related to whales, they're from the dolphin family. But dolphins are nice, playful and as far as I know, no one's ever been eaten by one. I don't think anyone has ever been eaten by an Orca in the wild, either.*

Suddenly, Stanley shouts with excitement, followed by Ivy screeching on the beach. I turn onto my back to look behind me just in time to see the Orca breaching the water only twenty or thirty feet from us. His magnificent body climbs into the air, glistening from the sun as it reflects off his shiny, smooth skin. A second later, he creates a mighty splash as he falls back into the sea, showering water over Stanley and me. The old man laughs with jubilation. "This is incredible."

*Yeah, easy for you to say. It's not your ass in the water.* Feeling completely vulnerable, I continue toward shore, swimming in rhythm with my heavy heartbeats. After a couple of minutes, the sea goes quiet, as does Stanley. Maybe that means the Orca have gone? With this in mind, I slow my pace and try to regulate my breathing. Ivy yells from shore and asks if she should call someone for the kayaker. Stanley yells to her that he'll make a call once on shore.

A massive flash of white appears in the dark waters in front of me, and as fast as it came, it disappears.

"Something is in the water," I say.

Stanley laughs. "There's a lot of things in the water, silly."

"No, something huge just swam in front of me. I saw it."

"There's nothing in these waters that can hurt you, girl."

If my father was here, he'd tell me that I was being a baby, especially since I've grown up near the water my whole life. I guess I should try to have a thicker skin. Maybe I've watched too many Shark Week episodes or oceanography programs since I've lived on the mainland. Whatever the reason, I'm scared, really scared right now.

"Paisley, look beside you," Stanley says, excitedly, pointing off to the right of me.

*I swear old man, if you're messing with me, I'm going to lose it once we're on solid ground.*

Then, I see it, just a few feet away from me. A killer whale.

The creature turns its body, revealing a huge eye below a glowing white spot on its head. He's checking me out. My head is shaking with fear as my teeth chatter and my hands shake. But then, something strange happens.

The creature and I make eye contact. Instantly, a calmness comes over me. His eyes are roughly the same size as a cow's, big and docile. The animal is curious, not vicious. As I watch him in the water, I see dorsal fins from the rest of the pod break through the waves. I stop and tread water, completely engulfed in a euphoric haze. At one point, an Orca swims under the kayak just inches from the hull…and me. I quickly submerge my head to try and catch a clear look. When my eyes adjust, I see three large Orca swimming beneath me, playfully weaving in and around each other. One of the creatures swims up to my foot and investigates. He's so close I can almost touch him.

When I can't hold my breath any longer, I come up for air. Stanley is leaning over the side and staring down at me. "What did you see?"

"They're underneath me. They're amazing, Stanley. Like huge sea-pups."

Stanley laughs and then points behind me to a shiny dorsal fin in the water. I turn and watch as the whales come to the surface, expel old air and breathe in new air before submerging again.

As much as I want to stay out here with my new playful friends, my legs are tiring quickly and I know that if I want to make it to shore, I should probably get moving. I swim toward the beach and Ivy, who now has a half-dozen spectators standing beside her, hoping to catch sight of the killer whales. As I swim, I think about what just happened. No matter how hard I try, I know I'll never be able to accurately describe to anyone the magic of this experience.

When I'm about twenty feet from shore, a man wearing Bermuda shorts and a sun hat wades out to help me haul in the kayak and Stanley. Ivy is there to meet me on shore, her face illuminated, like a kid at Disneyland. "I can't believe that you were right in the middle of them. They were all around you. How did it feel?"

I want to explain to her every emotion I'm feeling, but I can't. The only words that I can come out with right now are, "I felt free."

Once Stanley is settled on a log and someone loans him a cell phone, he waves, nodding his head in thanks as Ivy and I walk past. I don't want to stick around and answer a whole bunch of questions fromthe people on the beach. I want to be alone with Ivy and absorb the gift I was just given.

As we leave the beach, Ivy puts her hand on my shoulder. I look over at her. "Aren't you supposed to be mad at me?"

She shrugs. "Yeah, but it's hard to stay mad after witnessing such an incredible thing. Not to mention, you probably saved that old guy's life."

"Nah. I'm sure that someone would've eventually heard him and done the same thing that I did. It was no big deal." I don't want to seem smug.

Back in the main cabin, I find a box of KD in the cupboard. If I was hungry before, I'm starving now. After I microwave the cheesy pasta, I divide it onto two plates and carry them to the living room, then sit beside Ivy on the sofa. She doesn't turn on the TV, a definite hint that she wants to talk to me about something.

"You know, Paisley, I didn't mean to be cold to you all day," she says, looking down at her food. "It's just...when that girl called, it was like a punch in the stomach."

"I know. I felt the same way, trust me. But I didn't know she was going to call. I haven't spoken to her for over nine months."

Ivy nods and takes a forkful of food.

"But, since we're on the subject," I continue. My heart starts beating fast. "Why did you feel like you got hit in the stomach?"

She shrugs, looks up at me, and quickly swallows what's in her mouth. "This may sound super weird, since we've only been spending time one-on-one for a while, but I..." She pauses.

"What?"

"I think I'm falling for you." Ivy looks down again, vulnerable.

I smile. "I know what you mean."

Her eyes meet mine. "Now you know why I reacted the way I did."

I nodded "If the tables were turned, I'm sure I would've responded the same way." I reach over and put a hand on hers. "But just so we're clear, it's not Storm that I want, it's you." I'm shocked at my sudden burst of bravery.

She smiles, her cheeks pink. "So, back to the way we were then?"

"Absolutely," I say, leaning over her plate and kissing her on the cheek.

# Chapter Seven

The next day, we spend the morning hiking Nymph Falls. The weather is unpredictable, and we get periods of light showers, and we hide under trees and huddle until the sun comes back out. On the way home, Ivy turns the news channel on the radio. The forecast is calling for some high winds and they're expecting a lot of power outages. "Maybe we should stop and buy candles, just in case?" she says.

I agree and we stop by the General Store in Merville to load up on locally made candles. By the time we get home, the wind has already started gusting. Walking from the car to the house proves to be challenging—strong gales whip through the lot. Ivy and I laugh and hang onto each other as we walk up the stairs to the cabin.

"I hope these high winds don't last," she says. "We'll be confined to the house."

*Confined to the house with Ivy? I'd be happy.*

She tells me that she has about an hour of work to finish on the computer before we can do something together—play cards, watch TV or

103

lie in bed and read. Taking advantage of the time that she'll be busy, I go to the rentals to make sure all of the windows are closed and there aren't any power tools plugged in. As soon as I enter cabin 1, I hear Jasper clanking around in the back bedroom. Even though I know that he'd rather not talk to anyone, I feel it's my duty to inform him about the weather warning.

As soon as I step into the doorway of the back room, I see him standing on a step ladder and taping around the light fixtures.

"Jasper," I say, trying to get his attention. He doesn't turn around. "There's a strong wind warning and they're predicting power losses. Ivy and I bought candles and if you need any…"

"Why weren't these lights fixtures taped off?"

"I didn't know you were planning on painting the ceilings. I assumed that you were just going to do the walls and cupboards."

"That's the trouble with assuming. Most of the time, you're wrong."

"Look, I'm sorry, Jasper. I can do the other ones tomorrow, ok?"

"I guess so." He shrugs.

I slowly turn to leave the room, feeling uncomfortable. But before I can make it all the way out of the cabin, he calls after me.

"Yes?" I ask, turning around.

"My sister has taken ill," he says baldly. "She lives in Gold River and I need to go and help her for a week or so."

"Oh. I'm sorry she's sick. I'm sure you being there will cheer her up."

"We're pretty close, when we can see each other. I've probably let it go too long this time without dropping in."

I don't believe it. Is Jasper actually trying to converse with me? I'm completely blown away. I stay and chat with him for the next fifteen minutes, asking questions about his sister—what did she do before retiring? Does she have children? What's she like?

Jasper approaches each question with thought and care, doing his best to draw out his answers. By the way he's trying to engage me in conversation, it's apparent that he's feeling anxious over his sister and doesn't want to be alone.

"When are you planning on leaving?"

"Dawn's light, I suppose."

"Well, I'm sure you have more important things to do, preparing for your trip, but Ivy and I were planning on watching a movie and having some popcorn this evening. Did you want to join us?" I say, feeling obligated. After all, he's worked for my parents for years.

"Sounds good," he says, to my complete shock. He does his best to smile. "Six-ish?"

"That sounds great."

As soon as I'm finished battening down the hatches in the other cabins, I rush back to the main house to surprise Ivy with the news of Jasper coming over.

When I get to the office, Ivy is just finishing up on the computer. She tells me how our parents emailed from Florida and are having a great time, and how her father added a funny subject line to the email: *Have you two killed each other yet?* We both laugh.

Then, I share my news about Jasper. "You should have heard him. He was talking up a storm."

She stares at me for a few moments to make sure that I'm not pulling her leg. "Wow. There's a first. You think the old guy is finally slipping? I mean, he's the most impersonal man I've ever met."

"That's what I thought too. Maybe he's just feeling down about his sis and needs a distraction."

\* \* \*

We go downstairs to share the task of making a salad, something achievable that cooking-impaired girls like us can achieve. After we gather the veggies and cheese from the fridge, I wash each item and Ivy chops then puts everything in a big bowl. As the cool water flows over my hands, my mind reflects on being in the ocean with the killer whales. A shiver runs up my spine remembering how terrified I was at first. I thought for sure I wasn't going to survive the encounter until that Orca came up beside me and looked me in the eyes.

For some reason, my whale encounter reminds me of my father and the fear and lack of control I feel when I'm around him. Maybe I should do the same thing with Dad as I did when I was scared in the water. Maybe I should just let all my fear go and let nature take its course. Nothing I'm going to say or do is going to change how he's going to behave, so maybe I should just release the fear and the anxiety I feel when I'm around him. I have to do something, especially if I'm going to be stuck living in the same house with him for a while.

"What are you doing to those veggies? You're going to wash the color right off them," Ivy says with a laugh.

I look down at my hands and realize that I've been washing the same piece of lettuce repeatedly while I've been daydreaming. "I just want to make sure they're extra clean."

Ivy leaves the kitchen as I finish washing the food. A couple of minutes later, I hear the song *Light My Fire* by The Doors blare out of the speakers in the front room. Then, she walks into the kitchen and puts her arms around my back, moving close to me as I wash the vegetables. Her body gyrates in rhythm with the music. I laugh and sway my body in sync with hers. When all of the food is on the cutting board and my hands are dried, I turn and face her. She's smiling and her face is full of energy. "Dance with me, Paisley."

"I can't dance," I say, turning a bit red.

"Of course you can."

She takes a hold of my hands and slowly moves around in front of me. I follow her lead and copy her moves. I never knew she could be so spontaneous. This is not the Ivy I knew, conservative and predictable. This Ivy is exciting and fun. I grab onto her waist as she moves her body fluidly with the music. I pull her close and press my lips to hers. I'm feeling turned on and flushed. But she only kisses me briefly before she continues dancing. She's teasing me, and I like it.

The record finishes too soon and before I can suggest playing another one, Ivy looks at the clock on the wall and asks me what time Jasper is supposed to come over. I had forgotten all about him. My body temperature quickly returns to normal as I envision our evening with the old man.

We set the table and quickly eat before going upstairs and getting into some comfy movie-watching sweats. Back downstairs, Ivy grabs a bottle of wine from the cabinet and I microwave a few bags of popcorn. After we're organized and sitting on the couch, it isn't long before there's a loud rap on the door—Jasper. Ivy opens the door and Jasper walks in, wet and disheveled.

"It's an unforgiving evening out there," he says, finger-brushing his thinning crown.

"Have a seat," I say, motioning to the leather chair.

Jasper sits down, looking fidgety and uncomfortable, no doubt questioning his decision to come here and be social. Ivy offers him a glass of wine which he promptly accepts. Looking through the large DVD selection in the cabinet, I read each title aloud until I come across Blazing Saddles, a mock-Western that has a lot of laughs and is sure to help Jasper relax.

Before the movie has a chance to run through the opening credits, Jasper is on to his second glass of wine. Ivy puts the quickly emptying bottle on the coffee table and looks at me with a shrug.

The opening scene of the movie prompts a burst of laughter from our guest. Ivy and I look at each other and smile. I think that's the first time either one of us have heard him laugh out loud. When my father has told Jasper jokes in the past, he's simply smiled and nodded. I wish Dad was here to see him express himself so overtly.

As the show plays, Ivy and I take care not to sit too closely to one another. We don't want to reveal our newly found feelings for one another. Who knows how Jasper would react?

The movie doesn't disappoint, delivering non-stop comedic entertainment, prompting an assortment of snorts, guffaws and belly laughs from Jasper. At one point, Ivy gets up and retrieves a box of Kleenex so he can wipe his wet eyes. Halfway through the flick, Ivy and I are spending more time reacting to Jasper's outbursts than we are at the movie. When the movie is two-thirds over, I offer Jasper more wine, which he declines. Hopefully, he's feeling more relaxed around us now and doesn't need to be buzzed.

Just as the movie is ending, the electricity in the house wanes, causing the lights to fade and then brighten again.

"I expect we'll be losing power soon," Jasper says. "I guess I'd better be getting back to my shack." He gets up slowly and hands me his empty glass. "Thank you," he says, then walks to the front door.

"Do you need a flashlight or anything?" asks Ivy.

"No. I've worked on the property for so many years, I can find my way around without much trouble."

Ivy and I walk to the door and thank him for coming over. He nods. "I'll be leaving quite early in the morning to go to my sister's." He smiles, then—to my shock—he winks. "The two of you behave while I'm gone."

As soon as he opens the door, a gust of powerful wind pushes its way inside, carrying with it a spray of rain. Unfazed, Jasper walks off the porch and disappears into the dark night.

The moment we close the door, the power surges again. This time, it doesn't power up again. Instead, it shuts off completely.

Ivy suggests that we grab the flashlight and head to bed. I follow the beam of light as I walk behind her up the stairs. Thankfully, instead of going to my parents' room, she turns into mine and gets into bed. I slide in beside her and she immediately snuggles into me.

"Surprisingly, I had a really fun night tonight. I wasn't expecting Jasper to let loose the way he did." She giggles.

"I know. I thought his head was going to explode, he was laughing so hard. It was nice to see—it kind of changed my whole perception of him."

Ivy slowly starts stroking my arm, sending shivers over my skin. I turn onto my side and gently return the favor, rubbing her shoulders and caressing the silky skin on her neck. I can tell what I'm doing is turning her on by the slow moans she's making. I feel the warmth from her breath as she gets closer. She kisses me.

I taste the sweetness of the wine on her lips and I press my body closer to her. Her tongue meets mine as we kiss with hunger. Before long, our breathing becomes shallow and our hearts race, writhing in an erotic embrace on my small bed. Then, she sits up in the darkness and I hear her pull off her sweatshirt. I quickly follow suit, throwing mine to the floor. Lying back, I soon feel her warm, soft skin as her bare chest presses against mine.

I want her so badly, my body is shaking with anticipation. We kiss gently for a few moments, then she leaves my lips and ventures down my body, giving little kisses as she goes. My body arches in anticipation.

Then, out of nowhere, a loud series of bangs come from downstairs, pulling us both out of the moment.

"What was that?" Ivy asks, sitting up.

"It's probably just Jasper," I say, trying to catch my breath. "He must have forgotten something." Ivy rolls off me and I sit up. "Can I have the flashlight?"

After she passes it to me, I quickly scramble for my top, sliding it over my head as I stand. "Don't worry," I say. "I'll be back in a minute. Just stay here and whatever you do, don't fall asleep."

Ivy giggles and pulls the covers over her.

I shine the light down the stairs and walk to the front door. *Nice timing, Jasper.* I bet he forgot his keys, forgetful after the glasses of wine. I unlock the door and open it, shining the flashlight through.

Blinking in the harsh light is a very wet, very cold-looking, raven-haired female.

It takes me several seconds before I can speak. "Storm," I finally say, "what are you doing here?"

A crooked grin forms on her face. "I'm here to see you, silly."

"How did you get here?" I ask, trying to see behind her into the lot, but all I see is darkness.

"I thumbed my way up the island. Talked some old guy into veering off the main road to drive me here. It's amazing what some guys'll do if you show a little leg."

"Why are you here?" I say, still shocked. "When we spoke on the phone, I thought you understood that I didn't want to see you."

She folds her arms in front of her, trying to warm herself. "Paisley, we had such a beautiful thing once," she says. "I find it hard to believe that you'd let that all go."

Anger flares in my gut. "Storm, things are different now. I just went through nine months of being on the inside. Now that I'm out, all I want to do is forget the past and move on."

Her teeth are chattering now. "Can I at least come in? I'm freezing. And I did come all this way to see you in the middle of the night. I have no way out of here until the morning."

I sigh, knowing this was going to create a lot of static with Ivy and me. But I can't see another choice.

"Alright. Come in, but try to keep your voice down."

Storm walks past me. She's wearing tight jeans and the same short leather jacket she was wearing the night I met her. Her beautiful raven hair is disheveled and falling loose over her shoulders. She looks good, damn good.

It's instantly apparent to me that I still feel intimidated by her.

She sits in the chair and looks up at me with a smile. I step away from her and lean against the back of the sofa. I need to keep a safe distance from her. My knees are feeling weak and shaky, and I'm reminded again of the power she still has over me. Even though I am aware of how vulnerable I feel, I can't let her know it.

"You shouldn't have come, Storm."

"Why? You don't want to see me?" Her eyes are focused and sincere.

"Let's just say that the past is the past and I want to keep it that way."

Storm gets up and walks over to me. With the flashlight still in my hand, I point the beam toward the floor.

"You must've thought about me over the past nine months, Paisley. I sure thought about you."

"In what way?" I ask, letting curiosity get the better of me.

Even in the dark, I see the whiteness of her perfect teeth as she smiles. "I thought about all of those nights we spent making love. Pleasing one another. You were so shy, so innocent—it turned me on."

Feeling my temperature rise and my skin start to tingle, I take a deep breath to compose myself. She leans in until her lips are almost touching mine, her hot breath sweeping across my skin, causing me to salivate. "Do you remember the way I tasted?" Her voice is breathy and sensual.

I quickly move past her, my heart speeding and my hands clammy and wet. "Storm, I'm not the same person you met last year. I'm not innocent anymore. You saw to that."

"The jail thing?" she says, grabbing the flashlight out of my hand.

114

"Of course, the jail thing. You set me up. You ruined my life."

"Maybe that's why I'm here. Maybe I came to make it up to you."

"I don't want you to make it up to me, Storm. I just want my life back."

"I think you're wrong. I don't think you want your life to go back to the way it was. Not at all. You were a hermit, a recluse when I met you. Being with me made you want to break out of your shell. You went from an insecure girl to someone who wanted to taste, touch and feel everything, and you did." She reaches out and runs her hand through my hair.

Again, a warm flush runs over me. I need to stay focused and not let her get to me. I clear my throat and stand up straight. "Storm, how did you know that my parents weren't going to be here? You could've caused major shit if my father had answered the door, especially at this time of night."

"Maybe I'm psychic," she says with a laugh.

I glare at her, prompting her to give me a real answer.

"You know me, Paisley. I do my homework. I called and asked about reservations and whoever answered said that you were closed."

*Whoever answered? Ivy! Shit.*

Standing here with Storm, I completely forgot about Ivy. How come she hasn't heard

Storm and I talking and come downstairs yet? Or maybe she did hear us. My heart sinks.

"Storm, I can't stay here and talk with you. I have to go back upstairs."

"The girl that I spoke to on the phone. You're with her, aren't you?"

"It doesn't matter. That has nothing to do with anything. The truth is, seeing you now has only made me remember more clearly how you left me in prison to do time. Your time."

"You've got to let that go, Paisley. It's going to eat you up." She reaches for me.

I grab her hand to stop her, then reach down and take the flashlight. "You can stay in one of the rental cabins for the night. But in the morning, you're gone."

The room is quiet for a long moment before Storm speaks. "If that's how you feel. If you really don't want me to be here, I'll head back to Victoria in the morning."

I walk to the cabinet and take the keys for cabin number 1, then slide on my flip-flops at the front door. "Come with me. I'll take you over."

We walk together across the windy lot to the cabin. I quickly open the door and walk in, Storm following behind me. She heads over to the bed, then looks up at me. Her eyes are wide. "Will you sit with me for a second before you have to go? I'm kind of afraid to stay here all alone."

I sit on the bed and avoid eye contact with her. "You'll be fine out here, Storm. It's safe."

"I would feel a lot safer with you sleeping beside me."

"Good night, Storm." I get up.

She stands up quickly, and in one movement she grabs my shoulders and pulls me into her, pressing her perfect lips against mine.

It takes everything in me to pull away. "Stop. I won't do this again." I push away from her and hurry to the door.

"Fine," she says from behind me, laughing softly. "But I want you to do me a favor."

I stop at the door. "What's that?" I say, not turning.

"I want you to think of me while you're laying in bed tonight. Think about the passion we shared and think about all the crazy and fun times we had. If in the morning you feel the same way about us as you do right now, I'll gladly leave." She pauses. "But if you wake up feeling different...will you consider giving us another try?"

I open the door, and the wind swirls in. "Good night, Storm."

\* \* \*

When I'm back in the main house, I sit down on the sofa and try to process what just happened. I can't believe she showed up here. What was she thinking? If I meant as much to her as she's leading on, then why didn't she turn herself into the cops and tell the truth? Instead, she left me to rot in there, alone.

117

A wave of anger comes over me as I realise that, in all our words exchanged tonight, she had not said sorry. Not once. Typical Storm—she's never been accountable for anything she's done. With this in mind, the strong physical desire I have for her dissipates and I feel cold.

I slowly make my way up the stairs, not knowing what condition I'll find Ivy in. At the top of the landing, I turn off the flashlight and walk into my room, almost certain I'll find my bed empty with Ivy back in my parents' room.

* * *

As soon as I enter the bedroom, I hear the whistling of the wind outside as branches bang loudly on the windowpane. I look down at my small mattress and see Ivy wrapped up in my blanket, almost in the exact position I left her. I gently sit on the edge of the bed, trying not to wake her, then lie down next to her.

When my head touches the pillow, Ivy puts an arm around my waist and snuggles in close. "I'm sorry, Paisley," she says in a groggy voice. "I must have dozed off while I was waiting for you to come back. What took you so long? Did you get into a conversation with Jasper?"

"No, I didn't," I say, wishing that I could stop my answer there. But I know I can't. I have to tell her everything. I have no choice. In the morning she's going to see Storm at some point. It's better that I break the news to her now. I draw in a deep breath and muster my bravery. "Ivy, I've got to tell you something."

She groans. "Can it wait until morning? I just want to snuggle up with you and go back to sleep."

"I wish it could, but I think it's best that we talk now."

She yawns. "Ok. What is it?"

"Well, it wasn't Jasper at the door. It was...it was Storm."

Ivy says nothing. The only sounds in the room are from the weather outside. I wait for a few long moments. "Ivy?"

"You can't be serious." Her voice sounds surprisingly awake now.

"Unfortunately, I'm not kidding."

"This is bad, Paisley. There's no way this can end well."

"She promises to leave first thing in the morning."

"What does she want?"

"Guess."

"I hope you told her how you feel."

"Of course I did." I wrap my arm around Ivy's shoulders. "I'm sorry that she showed up out of the blue. Believe me, I just about freaked when I saw her."

"No shit!" Ivy says. "What a strange thing for her to do, show up uninvited all the way out here." She pauses. "I know she promised to leave in the morning, but I've got a bad feeling, Paisley."

"Don't worry. Everything will be back to normal tomorrow, you'll see."

When we cuddle together, I can feel the rigidness of Ivy's body next to mine. Though, I'm relieved that she didn't put the blame on me for Storm showing up. The last thing I want is for Ivy to pull away from me again.

As she drifts back to sleep, I lie awake and think about Storm. How taken I was with her the first night we met. It was the same kind of weather then as it is tonight, rainy and unpredictable. She is just as beautiful now as she was then. Maybe even more so. Pictures of our tumultuous relationship flash through my mind: the parties, the wild and spontaneous things we did, the sex—wow, the sex. Storm does everything in one speed—full on. She engulfs life with the same vigor as she does people, with ravenous hunger, devouring anybody or anything that strikes her fancy. That's what makes her so dangerous. And so irresistible.

* * *

With barely two hours sleep under my belt, I reluctantly sit up and rub my eyes. I look over at where Ivy was sleeping next to me, but the bed is empty. The early morning sun is shining in the window and illuminating the room. All I want to do is go back to sleep, but the last thing I want is for Ivy and Storm to meet without me being there. I don't trust Storm and with how confrontational Ivy can be, it's not a good idea for the two of them to be alone together.

With this in mind, I quickly get up and, after washing my face and straightening my hair a bit, I head downstairs. As soon as I enter the kitchen, the smell of freshly brewing coffee hits me. Ivy is standing over the sink with her back to me.

"Good morning, beautiful," I say.

"Hi. I'm just making some coffee and toast." She doesn't turn.

I walk up behind her and put my arms around her waist, giving her a gentle hug. "What should we do today?"

"Get rid of your friend."

"Point taken."

We don't talk much during our quick breakfast. I can tell by the look on Ivy's face that she's preoccupied with Storm being so nearby. Just as I'm putting my empty cup and saucer in the sink, there's a loud banging on the door.

"I'll get it," I say, heading toward the living room.

Ivy jumps up from the table and beats me to the front door. "Don't worry about it, I've got it."

As soon as she pulls open the door and sees Storm, her body goes rigid, like a cat encountering a stray dog. "Storm, I presume?" Ivy says, not masking her cold tone.

Storm grins at her as she steps through the doorway and holds out a set of keys. Ivy reaches out and grabs them, her eyes staying fixed on Storm's face. Tension rises to an unbearable level.

"I'm sorry, but I never caught your name," Storm says, with indifference.

"It's Ivy," I interrupt. "I told you before. Her name is Ivy." A gust of wind blows through the open door, and I busy myself with closing it.

Ivy glances at me and grins slightly before looking back at Storm. "Well, I guess I'd better let you two say your goodbyes. I've got a lot of work to do, and I'm sure you need to get going, Storm, considering the journey you have ahead of you."

Ivy leans over and kisses my cheek before heading up the stairs.

When she is out of sight, Storm laughs. "Wow, that was subtle."

"Yeah, she doesn't mince words," I say. "What you see is what you get. I guess that's what I like about her."

"Are you saying that I wasn't forthright with you while we were together?"

I stare at her with disbelief. "You're kidding, right? You were dealing drugs and guns and didn't even tell me. I had to get arrested before I was enlightened to all the shit you were into."

Her eyes flash with something. It could be guilt, or something else entirely. "I'm a changed person now. I know I've made my mistakes, Paisley. But I've learned from them."

"That's great," I say, not believing a word.

Storm steps toward me. "I know you miss me, Paisley," she says, her voice low. "I can feel it." She reaches out and strokes my arm. "I know when you're in bed, you're reminiscing about being with me, maybe even wishing you still were." She gestures to the floor above. "Your little friend Ivy is cute, but I don't believe for a second that you two share the passion that you and I did."

"You should get going," I say, using all of my will power to step away. "Ivy is right. You've got a long trip ahead of you."

Storm sighs loudly, then smiles. "Alright. Alright. You win. I'll back off. Give you some time." She pulls out a piece of paper, stepping close and tucking it into my jeans pocket. A hot flash cuts through my body. "Here's my cell number. Call me when you get tired of the boring little straight girl."

She walks to the door and opens it, her long black hair rippling down the back of the leather jacket. As she walks down the wooden steps, she turns to me and flashes me a beautiful smile, the same smile that pulled me in in the beginning. There's a flutter in my chest and my lungs feel heavy and tight. I watch as she walks down the lot toward the road, then I slowly close the door.

My forehead pressed against the door, I let out a deep, slow breath, my body trembling as the tension escapes. I resolve to stay there until I can get Storm out of my mind and refocus on what's really important to me now.

I turn and walk up the wooden stairs. Every step I take toward Ivy is one more step I get away from Storm.

# Chapter Eight

The morning sun casts a red hue across the shore as a light mist lingers over the calm sea. Ivy sits at the bow of the boat, dressed in a pair of blue jeans and a sweater, cradling a thermos of freshly brewed coffee. I watch as she shifts to get comfortable on the unforgiving aluminum seat, her hair wild and untamed as it blows freely in the wind.

I grasp the cool ridges of the throttle and provide a bit of gas. A small poof of smoke seeps out of the engine cover, followed by the strong odor of fuel. As the prop digs into the dense water, the bow lifts slightly, causing Ivy to lose her grip on the silver flask. It clanks to the boat floor before coming to a rest against my fishing rod, and I shoot her an apologetic grin. As we make our way across the strait, gulls resting on the water startle from the chatter of the 50-horsepower engine. The birds soar across the water, vanishing into the mist.

By the time we reach the southside bluffs off Savary Island, the mist has all but disappeared and has given way to a bright sun. I switch into neutral and throw my line out before putting the rod in the holder. Ivy looks beautiful with the sun lighting up her face and she gazes at the ocean, which is sparkling with sunlight.

"Are you having fun?" I ask, locking the reel.

"I feel more myself out here than I do anywhere else." she says, smiling looking over at the coastline. "One day, I'm moving to Texada Island or to Savary Island."

"And how will you support yourself in the middle of nowhere? It's not like these small islands will have a newspaper to write for."

She smiles at me. "I can work from anywhere, as long as I have an internet connection. I can submit my work online." She takes a sip of coffee. "And what about you, Paisley?"

I laugh. "Naw, I'm a terrible writer. That wouldn't work for me."

She shakes her head. "I meant, where would you like to live and work?"

"I don't know. I mean, I love the area. I guess the only issue is that I don't want to live close to my father. I don't think I'm strong enough to be within reach of his disapproving remarks. I would go crazy."

"You wouldn't be near him if you lived on one of these islands. I can't see him taking the boat over just to torment you." She winks.

As the skiff bobs and bounces in the water, I look south to Texada, a beautiful little island that has about 1,200 inhabitants and only two small stores. Our family doctor used to live over there. He talked about the place a lot, making it sound like a hidden paradise with lakes, waterfalls and beautiful trails.

It would be nice not to live in the cement jungle of Vancouver. I had chronic headaches there. I was never sure if they were caused by all the sounds of living in an urban setting or if it was the pollution in the air. Either way, aspirin was mandatory on my grocery list.

As I turn the bow to face the small swells, lessening the rocking of the skiff, I think about what it would be like, sharing a space with Ivy, somewhere beautiful where we could be alone.

"What's the grin for?" Ivy asks.

I suck on my lips and look over at the rod, trying to divert an answer. "No bites yet. Maybe I don't have enough line out."

"Why are you even fishing? It's not like either one of us is going to cook whatever you catch."

"You're right." I laugh. "That's why I'm using barbless hooks, to catch and release. For me, it's all about the experience of being out here."

She looks out at the ocean again. "I hear ya."

We spend the next hour in front of the bluffs, until the wind picks up and the swells grow, heaving the small boat around. Ivy looks uncomfortable as I try to keep us from crashing into the rocks.

"I guess we should head back," I say, raising my voice above the rumble of the wind.

Ivy nods as she grips the sides of the boat. I quickly wind in the line on the reel, place the rod against the seats and power up in the direction of home.

* * *

We drag the skiff up the shore to dry land, where I throw the tarp overtop and place a few large stones around it so it doesn't blow away. Toting the rod and thermos, we push against the wind as we head toward the house.

Once inside, we wash up and collapse on the sofa. She looks over at me, her cheeks red from the hot summer sun. "Thanks for a great little outing. It was fun," she says, putting a hand on my leg.

I raise an eyebrow. "Are you trying to flirt with me?"

"No way. What kind of a girl do you think I am?"

I lean over and kiss her softly. Her lips are warm and wanting. Then she leans back and smiles at me. "You don't want to start this now, do you? We've got to save something fun for later."

I sigh. I'm already starting to feel worked up and flushed, but I know that we should probably do something productive while the sun is still up. "I've got a few things to do in the cabins today. I'll make us some KD and then I'll work for a while."

"Can I come and help you in the rentals? I've finished most of my online work, so I don't really have much to do."

I smile at the thought of her tagging along. "Well, it's kind of boring work, but you're welcome to come along."

We quickly make and devour Kraft Dinner before heading out to the rentals. In the first cabin, I take the tape off the window frames and light switches where Jasper has painted while Ivy folds up the drop cloths. Then Ivy finds a sticky note with Jasper's messy writing: *Paisley, I need you to scrape the paint off the window frame in the bedroom so I can paint it when I get back.* We spend ten minutes searching the rooms for the scraper before deducing that it's not in the cabin. We lock it up and head to the small shed, where there are plenty of rollers and drop cloths and tape, but still no scraper.

"Why don't we walk up to Jasper's shack and see if he left it there?" Ivy says.

Hand in hand, we stroll up the long, winding trail to the small cabin where Jasper has lived for as long as I can remember. I've never purposely walked up here before. I was always a little afraid of bumping into the old grumpy codger.

After a few minutes of walking, the small red building comes into view. It's about the same size as a big shed, with paint-chipped window frames and a rickety, faded yellow door. I remember my dad offering to let him live in one of the rental cabins, but apparently he prefers to be out here in the woods, away from people all together.

"That scraper better be around here somewhere," I say, walking up the rickety narrow steps.

Ivy notices a bucket just beside the front window. As she looks inside the pail, I try the front door. It's locked. "Find anything?" I ask, watching her riffle through the pail.

"Nothing."

I walk back down the steps and over to where she is standing. "Now what?" I ask, feeling frustrated.

"No idea," she answers, shifting her attention to the window on the front of the shack.

"What are you thinking?" I glance at the window.

"Maybe he left the scraper on the sill?"

"Well, it's way too high up to tell, and it'd be weird for him to put the scraper there. I mean...he would've had to have a ladder."

Ivy shrugs and walks up to the wall of the shack, putting her hands against the wood and looking up. "I'll boost you up so you can look on the sill."

The idea doesn't thrill me, but then I remember her stubborn streak and decide that it's probably just easier to go along with her idea. She crouches over and braces her back against the wall then interlocks her hands together. "Ok, put your foot up on my hands.

Once you're up, you can stand on my shoulders and have a look at the sill."

"You're crazy, Ivy," I say, shaking my head and laughing.

I take off my trainers so I don't get her all dirty, then slowly place my foot into her hand. I lift myself up and grab onto her shoulders to even out my weight. I hear her grunt under the strain. I steady myself on the wall as I step onto her shoulders, then straighten up and grasp the edge of the frame, pulling myself up as high as possible.

"Is it there?" she asks.

"I'm not high enough up to see. I need more height."

Ivy sighs loudly. "Just stand on my head."

"Huh?" I ask, wondering if I heard her right.

"Do it, Paisley. I've got a really strong neck."

I'm not sure if it was the thought of our feeble human pyramid or the absurdity of what she just said, but I can't help it. I burst into laughter.

As soon as she hears me, Ivy starts to giggle and vibrate, weakening her body. She wavers back and forth, and I clutch the thick sill harder, trying to right myself. It's no use— Ivy has now broken out into choking laughter and every bit of strength is gone. She folds in half and my feet slide down her back. Thankfully, I'm able to keep my grip on the window frame and I'm left swinging back and forth like a wind chime against the building.

"Ivy, get it together," I giggle. "Seriously. I don't know how long I can hold on."

She tries hard to compose herself. "Oh no, Paisley. Shit! Just hang on, let me find something I can stand on."

"What about the bucket?" I say, my voice straining.

"Great idea," she exclaims, grabbing the pail and dumping the contents on the ground.

She quickly turns the pail upside down and pushes it close to the wall before standing on it and grabbing the back of my legs. "Ok. I'm going to turn around, put my back against the wall and you can step on my shoulders and then slowly get down."

Oh no, not the shoulder thing again. A quick vision of Ivy and me in a tangled heap on the ground flashes through my mind. Still, I don't have many options. Ivy presses her back against the wall and guides each of my feet to her shoulders. Slowly, I loosen my grip on the wood and place my hands flat on the wall. Ivy talks me calmly through each step: "Ok, you're doing great, now bend down and…"

And then, a loud, unmerciful crack sounds out, and Ivy yells and jerks. As fast as I can, I reach up and just barely manage to grab the windowsill before she disappears from under me, and I'm left swinging again as I strain to place my other hand on the narrow ledge.

"What happened?" I ask, gasping.

"The freakin' bucket broke."

"Oh no. Now what?" I say, my aching hands quickly weakening.

She struggles to free her legs from the bucket. "Hey, there's a stump. I'll just roll it over here. Stay put."

Like I was planning on scaling the building or something.

"I can't hang on," I say, starting to panic.

Ivy walks over and pushes up on my feet with her hands. A small amount of pressure releases in my tired fingers.

"Try to pull yourself up so you can rest on your forearms on the ledge, Paisley. That way all the weight won't be on your hands."

"There's no way I can pull myself up that far."

"Yes, you can, Paisley. Just think about gym class and doing those stupid chin ups."

"I hated those damn things," I say, grabbing a good hold of the sill.

"Ok, just do it now. I'll help. Just give it all you can."

She went from fumbling fool to motivational speaker in two seconds. I take a deep breath and picture gym class, looking up at that long silver chin-up bar. I close my eyes and envision Miss Young, the cranky gym teacher glaring at me, waiting impatiently for me to fail. I was never good at anything athletic. Still, I never failed at doing chin-ups, especially when Young was watching. I focus hard until her disapproving face is clear in my mind then take a long full breath. With everything I have, I pull my body upward until my right elbow is on top of the windowsill. I muster what's left of my upper body strength and pull as hard as I can until my other elbow is level with the first. I quickly lock my hands around my forearms and lay them on the narrow ledge. My body feels much more secure in this position.

"You did it, Paisley!" Ivy screeches excitedly. "I'm going to get the stump now."

As Ivy leaves the front of the building to retrieve the stump, my eyes focus through the dirty windowpane. The first thing I notice is a small cot-like bed. Then I see an old dresser pushed up against a wall with books and junk stacked on top. "I think this window goes to Jasper's bedroom," I call to Ivy.

"Well, tell me what you see, it'll take the situation off your mind," she says, grunting as she rolls the stump.

I concentrate once more on the tiny room. There are pictures on the wall, all of landscapes and flowers and stuff—typical old people décor. Then, my eyes wander to a larger picture on the floor, perched against the closet doors. I have to look twice and focus hard before my mind believes what my eyes are seeing. "I don't believe it. He actually has a picture of Madonna in there."

"Huh?"

"You heard me right. Why would he have a picture of Madonna? It makes no sense."

"Do you mean *The* Madonna, as in the Virgin Mary?"

"Nope. I mean *Madonna*, as in cone tit bras and fishnet stockings."

Suddenly, I can't hear the stump rolling anymore.

"You're teasing me," she says.

"I'm telling you, Ivy. Jasper has a picture of the singer, Madonna, in his room."

"That's so weird. I don't get it. What else do you see in there?" The rolling resumes.

Peering back inside the window, I scan the room for further oddities. I spot a small bookcase against the far wall. On the shelves, I see a Raggedy Andy doll, a Rubik's Cube and a baseball—strange items for an old man to collect. I hear the stump hit the cabin wall.

"Ok, Paisley. I'm going to get on the stump."

Ivy grabs one of my legs and places it on her shoulder. Slowly, I step on her other shoulder with my other leg. Before I know it, I'm free of the ledge and standing beside her on the stump. I shake out my aching arms and breathe a sigh of relief.

"That was interesting," she says, wiping her hands on her shirt and grinning. "Did you find the scraper?"

I shake my head and laugh as I hop off the stump and onto solid ground. "Jasper probably has it in the back of his truck or something."

As we walk down the path toward home, Ivy starts laughing. "Madonna? Really?"

"Yeah. It was weird to see, for sure."

"Why would he have a picture of her?"

"I don't know, Ivy. Maybe he looks at it when he's in bed and having happy time."

Ivy stops. "Thanks for that image, Paisley. I may never have sex again."

I laugh and grab her hand, tugging so she starts walking again. "Just kidding. I don't know why he has the picture. Maybe a tourist that was renting a cabin left it in their room."

"Yeah, I guess that would make sense. But I wouldn't have kept it. I would've thrown it out."

"You don't like Madonna?"

"I did until she said Canada is boring."

"Yeah, I heard something about that while I was in jail. Most of the inmates were pretty disgusted."

"And now I'll never be able to look at Jasper without thinking of her."

We giggle as we walk the rest of the trail and onto the main lot. I tell Ivy that I'll take one more look in the rental cabin and then I'll meet her at the main house. I watch her perfect body sway as she makes her way toward the steps, but when she glances back, I look away. I don't want her to catch me staring.

Once I've done another quick scan for the scraper and come up empty, I tidy up and lock the door. On my walk to the house, I catch myself grinning as I picture how ridiculous Ivy and I must have looked trying to rescue me from

136

the ledge. It's a funny memory we can laugh at down the road. Maybe even years from now.

Night crawls over the horizon and across the shore. Ivy and I share a salad while watching Family Guy reruns. After an hour or two, Ivy says she's tired and that she's going upstairs to have a bubble bath.

Putting on a blues compilation record of my dad's, I lie back on the couch with my feet on the coffee table and close my eyes, picturing Ivy as she disrobes and slowly sinks into the hot water. My face instantly flushes and my skin tingles.

Just as the first song on the album ends, I hear her call from upstairs: "Paisley, can you come here for a minute? And turn up the tunes."

I jump up and quickly crank the volume. She probably wants me to grab her robe or something. I climb the stairs, wondering how much of her will be revealed when I step inside the steamy room.

When I reach the top of the landing, there are no lights on anywhere, just the small flicker of candlelight coming from the slightly open door to the bathroom. My heart flutters as I slowly walk toward the room. I hear the splash of water, like she's gently washing herself. As I push the door open, I drop my gaze to the floor, not wanting her to think I was disrespecting her privacy. "You called me?" I ask, focusing on the muffled music playing downstairs. "Did you want something?"

"Yes," she says huskily. "I'm feeling kind of lonely in this big old tub all alone. I thought maybe you would join me."

I look up and across to the tub. Her hair is in a messy bun and her knees are pulled up to her chest. The soft glow from the candle illuminating her perfectly. I smile and slowly begin pulling off my shirt. As she watches me, I suddenly become very aware of how perfect her body is and how imperfect mine is.

Ivy notices my shyness. "Does it make you uncomfortable that I watch you?"

"No. I mean, I don't know."

"Do you want me to look away?"

"No," I say, not making eye contact.

"You're beautiful, Paisley. Don't you know that?"

"You're the one that's beautiful, Ivy. Not me."

She snickers. "Thanks, but that's not the way I see it."

I finish taking off the rest of my clothes, then walk slowly over to the tub and step in the hot water. When I'm seated, Ivy grabs my ankles and pulls me toward her. Her face is glowing from a combination of candlelight and steam. She leans into me, smiles and laughs before pressing her wet lips against mine. Our tongues gently caress each other's.

It isn't long before my heart rate has elevated and I'm hot, wet and out of control. Simultaneously, we decide to continue our physical conversation on the bed, my parents' bed. My father's face flashes through my mind and I smile.

We spend the rest of the night exploring each other and experiencing incredible tandem orgasms. Finally, in the early hours of the morning, my beautiful Ivy and I fall asleep in each other's arms—euphoria.

* * *

The early sun floods the room with a soft warm glow. Ivy is spooning me, her legs intertwined with mine. My mouth is dry, and my first instinct is to get up and get a glass of water but I'm afraid if I move, I'll wake her. I close my eyes, hoping that I'll drift back to sleep in our perfect embrace, but only seconds pass before I feel her legs twitch and she slowly wakes.

A few moments later she's unhooked herself from my legs. I sit up beside her and rub her warm back. She leans over and kisses me. We wake together, talking about our magical evening and then discussing what our plans are for the day. We settle on going to Courtenay to get groceries. Afterwards, we'll spend a quiet evening sharing a nice take-out dinner and watching a movie or playing cards.

* * *

The drive to Courtenay is great—a perfect summer day with Ivy in the convertible. The wind is warm and soft as it twists and lifts our hair.

At Superstore, Ivy playfully taps my butt with her foot as I push the cart down the aisles. As we coast along, both of us grab instant meals by the handful and put them in the cart. By the time we hit the till, our total is well over a hundred bucks.

"Not only are we the world's worst cooks, but apparently our shopping habits are left wanting, too," Ivy says, laughing.

"I think we did pretty good. I mean, at least we got salad, right?"

After we pack the groceries into the trunk, I take the cart back while Ivy starts the car. I'm smiling as I click the buggy into the one in front and retrieve my quarter.

Just as I turn to walk back to the car, I notice a woman sitting in a small, red compact. She has dark, shoulder-length hair, and is staring at me.

Because of the reflection of the sun, I can only somewhat make out her features. Why is she gawking at me? She hasn't moved her head once.

As I pass in front of her, I get a clearer view through the side window. Our eyes meet, and I get a strong shiver through my body. There's something familiar about this woman.

When I get back to Ivy's car, I turn and look back at the red compact, but it's gone. Getting in, I do up my seatbelt and scan the lot.

"What's wrong?" Ivy says, shifting into reverse.

"Nothing," I say, forcing a grin. "Everything's great."

"Nice try, Paisley. I know you too well—I can tell when something is bothering you. What is it?"

I sigh. "Honestly, I don't know. When I put the buggy back, I turned to see this woman gawking at me. She just kept staring. And she looked familiar, but I couldn't place where I knew her from. It was weird."

Ivy laughs. "Well, of course she was checking you out. I'd check you out too."

"I'm serious, Ivy. She creeped me out."

"Was it Storm?"

"No. It definitely wasn't her—a completely different person."

"Then don't worry about it, sweetie."

"I guess you're right," I say with a shrug.

Ivy turns on the stereo, which gives me time to get the weird incident out of my mind. By the time we pull into the lot, I've convinced myself that the woman was probably someone I didn't like when I went to school here. I definitely knew enough of those girls, ones that disapproved of me because I wasn't in the right crowd—I was a bit of a rebel.

While Ivy and I put the groceries away, I think again of the woman, which prompts me to remember my high school days here in the valley. How horrible that time was for me. It was when my father and I really started to fight a lot. The space grew between us, and it wasn't long before we were barely speaking to each other.

I sigh and Ivy looks at me. Quickly I try to cover my sudden bummed-out mood.

"What movie should we watch tonight?" I say, amping up my voice to sound cheery.

"We'll find something, I'm sure," says Ivy, putting two frozen meat pies in the oven.

* * *

The movie selection is pretty hurting. There's only an old Western or a Harlequin movie to choose from, so we opt for the western. Snuggling together on the sofa, we steal the odd kiss but mostly we just lie together.

I'm not sure if it was the fresh air or the incident at the store that prompted me to dive headfirst into painful memories involving my dad, but I feel exhausted when the show ends. Ivy makes us both a cup of tea and puts on an old 60's compilation album, one I don't remember Dad playing before. As the moody R&B songs play, we continue to snuggle. After a few songs, I start to nod off. Ivy is yawning too, which tells me it's going to be an early night.

Again, we opt to sleep in my parent's bed, but instead of fooling around, we face each other lying down and gently caress one another's skin. As I look in her eyes, there's no question—I love this girl. I don't care what I end up doing down the road. As long as Ivy is with me, I'll be happy.

* * *

The sound of something smashing wakes me.

I can hear the cadence of Ivy's deep breathing in my ear. My brain tells me the noise downstairs was nothing more than a broom falling over or something. Still, my gut would feel better if I check it out.

I quietly slip out of bed, trying not to wake Ivy from her peaceful sleep. As I leave the dark bedroom, the hallway to the stairs is even darker. Fearing the bright light will wake Ivy, I let my feet guide me to the top of the stairs, then use my hand on the wall to stabilize myself as I walk slowly down the wooden steps.

Just as I reach the halfway point, I hear a slow creaking sound, like a door being opened. Then I feel a sudden blast of outside air push against me.

A chill runs through my bones and I stop dead in my tracks. Is the front door open? But how would that be possible? I locked it myself before we went to bed. I try to tell myself that maybe one of the downstairs windows was left open. Maybe Ivy opened one after we got back from Courtenay. After all, it was a warm day.

I force air into my tensed lungs and try to regulate my breathing. I'm being a baby. As my dad would say, *buck up and don't be such a*

143

*chicken shit.* With his words in my head, I continue down the stairs.

When I reach the bottom floor, I run my hands over the wall, feeling for the light switch. Just as I flick on the light, I hear a clacking sound coming from the kitchen. The shiver returns to my bones. My feet move slowly toward the door as the noise continues. Did an animal somehow get inside? I extend my hand and slowly push the door open.

The light from behind me shines into the kitchen and onto the clacking shutters in the open window. I exhale and drop my shoulders. As I guessed, Ivy must have opened the window and forgot to close it.

I smile as I flick the kitchen light on and walk over to the window. I grab the top of the window and am just about to push it down when I hear the faint sound of music coming from the living room.

I quit moving and listen harder in case my mind is playing tricks on me. Sure enough, I hear the barely audible noise of a melody.

Knowing that Ivy is fast asleep upstairs, and the music wasn't playing when I came down, there's no doubt in my mind now—someone uninvited is in the house.

With my heart rate accelerating, I look around the kitchen for anything I can use to defend myself. I quickly focus on the knife block and tip toe toward it. Trying to be silent, I slowly slide the biggest knife out of the wood and turn toward the kitchen door, sliding my feet quietly across the linoleum. All I can hear now is the booming of my heart in my chest.

Using my now shaking fingers I gently push on the door. The first thing I see is the spinning record on the stereo. I quickly scan the room, looking for the intruder, but can't see anyone. As I take a tiny step into the living room, the kitchen door creaks behind me. I hold my breath until the door finally settles in place and is silent once again. Looking down at the long silver blade in my trembling hand, I wonder what to do. Should I run upstairs and wake Ivy?

I decide to investigate a little further before I wake her.

I tiptoe toward the front bay window to check behind the long heavy curtains. My legs are starting to shake. Inside, I feel like a child winding up a jack in the box and waiting for the clown to come springing out. I hated those damn things; they scared the hell out of me. I feel the draft on my legs as I near the front window. Slowly, I reach out and grasp the thick drapes. Holding my breath, I slowly draw back the heavy fabric. Every hair on my body stands on end when I see my reflection in the window. I look petrified as I firmly grasp the long shiny blade.

I keep pulling the curtain on the squeaky track when my attention shifts to the sound that's softly playing. I finally recognise the song.

*My Girl* by the Temptations.

A shiver runs up the back of my neck. I grasp the knife tighter and turn around. The intruder stands only a bit taller than me. Her eyes are crazy-looking, a severe green, looking right through me.

"What the hell are you doing here, Storm?" I whisper.

"I had no choice, Paisley. Some crazy men are chasing me. I had nowhere else to go."

"The open window? *My Girl*? Why didn't you just knock, or better yet, call me?"

"I don't have a phone. As for knocking, I didn't want you to open the door and cause a big scene. They might hear us."

"Who might hear us?"

"The men that are trying to kill me. They think that I owe them money, but it's not true. I don't owe them anything!"

"What the hell is going on down there?" Ivy calls from the top of the stairs.

"It's nothing, Ivy," I holler back. "Go back to bed. I'll be right there."

"Sorry, have I interrupted happy time?" Storm says, sarcastically.

"What do you want, Storm?" I say, my temperature rising.

"I told you, I'm scared, and I didn't have anywhere else to go."

Suddenly, I hear Ivy's voice, much closer than before. "I call bullshit." I whirl to see her at the bottom of the stairs, her eyes flashing.

Storm looks at her, her eyes dark and severe. "What's that supposed to mean?"

146

Ivy takes a step closer. "What I mean is, Victoria is a hell of a long way away. If someone is chasing or following you, why would you come this far up island?"

Instead of answering Ivy, Storm turns her eyes back to me. "Paisley, I only came up here because I needed to be with someone I trust. It's not like I could go to the cops or anything. The guys that are after me would blow my head off."

"So, what do you expect us to do about it?" I ask.

"Just let me stay one night. When morning comes, I'll be out of here. I promise."

Ivy walks up and puts her arm around me. Storm glares at her.

I turn to Ivy. "We're going to be here all night unless we let her have the cabin to sleep in," I mutter.

Ivy shifts her eyes from mine to Storm's. "Well, I don't think it's a good idea, but whatever gets her out of here faster."

Storm scoffs. "Gee, thanks. That's really sweet."

Ivy kisses my cheek, then slowly heads back up the stairs. "This bullshit has got to stop," she says over her shoulder. "After tonight, we don't want to see you around here again."

Storm scoffs again and shakes her head, glancing back at me.

For a moment, I look into her eyes, remembering how her beauty once had such a strong power over me. She knew it too. That's how she manipulated me. And her lips—her full, perfect lips I always longed to kiss—now seem like nothing more than small doors to lies and deceit.

For the first time since the day I met her, I feel nothing.

"Well," I say. "Since you've gone to all of the trouble of breaking into our home, I guess we have no choice but to accommodate you for a night. Just understand, Storm, if you ever show up here again, there will be a much different outcome. Even if you have a thousand men chasing you."

Her eyebrows pull together. "You don't believe me?"

"It's not that I believe you or I don't, it's that I just don't care anymore. But yeah, I don't really believe you, either. If someone is chasing you, I highly doubt they would follow you this far up island, like Ivy said."

She shakes her head. "Whatever, Paisley. Believe what you want."

* * *

As soon as I open the door to cabin #2 and we walk in, Storm reaches out for my arm. I pull away. She drops her hand, looking disgusted.

"Well, I guess she's completely beguiled you. I can see that you have nothing left for me. That hurts, Paisley."

"First of all, nobody has beguiled me. Secondly, cut the shit. If you ever gave a damn,

148

you wouldn't have done what you did to me. I think this whole obsessive thing is a result of you losing your control over me."

"I can't believe that you really think that. I'm crazy about you."

I chuckle as I grab onto the door handle. "Tomorrow morning, when you get up, leave the key on the bed and please—stay the hell away from me."

"If that's really what you want," she says, slumping down onto a chair. Her eyes are glistening as she looks at me. "I love you, Paisley."

I force myself to look away. "No, Storm, that's a lie. I think the only thing you and I ever had in common was that we both loved you." I step out and shut the door behind me.

As I make my way over to the house, I feel a heavy weight lift from my shoulders. I smile as I walk up the stairs and through the front door.

When I slide into bed, Ivy twists and looks at me. "Did you have much trouble with her?"

"No," I say, running my fingers through her hair. "I think she finally gets it."

"And you?" Ivy says, inching closer toward me.

"And me what?" I ask, brushing a wisp of hair out of her eyes.

"How do you feel? I mean..." She takes a deep breath. "I understand if you still feel something for her."

I stare into her eyes. "I can honestly say, I feel nothing. I don't even pity her. All I felt when I looked at her tonight was…" I pause to find the word. "Disgust."

Ivy smiles and kisses me. "Good."

We kiss one another tenderly and wrap our bodies together in a warm embrace, falling asleep in each other's arms.

# Chapter Nine

The sound of car tires on gravel shakes me out of my dream. As soon as I open my eyes, I see the reflection of head lights panning across the window. I look over at the digital clock on the bedside table, 3:15 AM.

*Who in the hell would be here at this hour?* I sit up and try to focus. Ivy sits up beside me. "What's going on?" she asks, rubbing her face.

"No idea." I slide out of bed and pad to the window, squinting out. There's a car, a dark sedan in the courtyard. They are slowly driving in front of the cabins.

Ivy gets out of bed and stands next to me. "Who is that?"

"Like I said, I have no idea."

We keep watching as the vehicle pulls up to Cabin #2 and stops. When the engine turns off, the lights go out and all we see are two dark figures getting out of the car and walking to the cabin door.

I can't remember if I locked the door when I left Storm earlier, but the men seem to have no problem gaining entry. When the door opens, the light from inside shines on both men. One is

151

about six feet tall, with broad shoulders and short dark hair. The other man is leaner and has shoulder-length, dark hair.

"What should we do?" Ivy whispers.

"I don't know." My mouth is dry. "Maybe they're friends of Storm's. Maybe they came to give her a ride back to Victoria."

The door closes behind the men and all we can make out are shadows passing behind the curtains. Ivy fumbles in the darkness and finds her jogging pants, which she puts on while leaning against me. I keep my eyes fixated on the cabin, waiting for any signs of Storm.

It's a bit chilly by the window, so I ask Ivy to hand me a sweater or whatever she can find. After a minute, she presses an item of clothing in my hand. It's too dark to see what she gave me and I don't want to turn on any lights while there are strangers outside. I'd rather see them without them seeing us. I try and maneuver the piece of clothing over my head and arms, my fingers getting caught in the loose knit. Then the scent of my mother hits me. Ivy must have pulled this out of one of my mom's drawers.

Ivy is just about to say something when the door to the cabin opens and a stream of light shines out onto the ground. The first person through the doorway is the tall, thin guy. Right behind him is the larger man with the short hair who has Storm by one of her wrists and is pulling her outside.

"What in the hell?" Ivy says, not whispering any more. "Paisley, she was telling the truth. Those are the men."

I nod as I keep my eyes fixated on the trio below.

"What should we do?" her voice has a tinge of panic.

"I don't know," I say, feeling stunned as my own panic runs through me.

"We've got to call the cops. I mean, what if they kill her?"

As much as I want Storm out of my life for good, Ivy is right. We have to do something.

I watch as Storm squirms and tries to yank her arm free from the goon. It doesn't appear to be working. The guy is too big and strong. When he lifts his arm, Storm rises to her tiptoes. She's like a rag doll under his strength. The thin man goes to the passenger side of the sedan and the interior light comes on. I see him reach into the glove compartment and grab something before closing the car door and walking over to Storm and the brute. The men appear to say something to one another and then they start walking to the house.

"Paisley. They aren't taking her away in their car, they're coming toward us. We've got to go downstairs and get our phones."

I lead the way to the stairwell, banging my shin hard on the corner of the bed frame. Normally I would be hollering from the pain but right now my adrenaline is suppressing anything

I'd normally feel. Ivy grabs the back of my shirt as I guide us down the steep staircase.

"Hurry, Paisley."

"I'm doing my best. It's pitch black in here," I hiss. "Just grab onto the railing and watch your step."

"My cell is plugged into the outlet on the living room counter. Where's yours?"

I have to think for a moment before I remember plugging my phone in beside hers before we went to bed, "It's on the counter. Just hang onto me again when we hit the bottom. I'll lead us to the cabinet."

We are only a few feet from the bottom of the stairs when we hear the sound of scuffling outside of the front door.

"Hurry," Ivy says, almost sobbing.

I run my hands over the wall and step quickly across the room with Ivy firmly grasping on to the back of my shirt. Finally, I feel the edge of the counter with my shaking fingers. We're almost there.

"Once we get the phones, I'm going to try and find the back door, ok?" I whisper.

"No, Paisley. I'm too scared to go outside. Let's just go back upstairs and call the…"

Her words are lost as thunderous cracking fills the room. Both Ivy and I stop in our tracks, both of us too terrified to breathe. Again, the loud crack cuts through the living room, only this time, it's followed by the sound of the front door swinging open and hitting the wall behind it. A cold, terrifying gust of air pushes into us, accompanied by the voice of one of the intruders: "Find a light switch."

They can't see us yet, it's too dark in here. I quickly move backwards until I bump into Ivy. I reach behind me and grab her hand. I've got to get her out of here before the men see us. This may be our only window to escape.

"Let me go, you stupid pig," Storm snarls. "I told you, I haven't got your money." We hear sounds of her scuffling on the floor only feet from where Ivy and I are pressed up against the wall. I push on Ivy, motioning her to back up but she doesn't move. Her body is stiff, petrified.

Then, the light flicks on and all the oxygen leaves my body.

Standing just feet in front of us are the two men and Storm, bent over in a prisoner's clench as the larger thug grips the back of her neck. This is the first time I have seen her vulnerable and out of control.

"What the hell is going on here? What do you want?" I say, my voice cracking with fear.

"I told you already," Storm chokes out. "They want their money that I never stole."

"Shut up, bitch!" says Storm's captor. He pushes her in our direction, and she lands on her knees in front of us.

Ivy grabs onto my arm. I can feel her body shaking through her cold, stiff hands. I put my hand over hers to calm her, even though I'm panicking inside. Storm scrambles to her feet and turns to face the thugs. "You sonofabitches.

How dare you. You are going to regret coming after me."

"Who are you?" Ivy says, on the verge of crying.

"The large one with no neck is Thorn," Storm says harshly. "As in thorn in my ass. The thinner one is his bitch, Wolf."

The thinner man lunges at Storm and backhands her across the face. She lands on her side and pulls her knees to her chest, groaning.

I look down at Storm and then up at the two men. "Please, just leave. We have no money here and I'm almost positive that Storm doesn't have any, either."

The larger man, Thorn, snickers. "I think you're right, Paisley."

"How the hell does he know your name?" says Ivy quietly.

Then it occurs to me, *Yeah, how does he know my name?*

"How do you know her name?" Ivy asks, moving closer to me.

"I'm fucking psychic, Ivy. Any more questions?"

"So, what's it gonna be, boys?" Storm says, sitting up and wiping blood from her lip. She smiles as she examines the red streaks on her hand. "Are you going to have your way with us or just slap us around?"

Thorn grins. "Maybe both."

"Actually," Wolf interrupts. "I'm not interested in your bodies. What I want is the fucking money." He reaches into the back of his pants and pulls out a silver handgun.

My knees go weak and my heart starts thumping. As I begin to hyperventilate, my head spins and I feel like passing out. I fight hard to keep my bearings. I need to stay strong for Ivy, who is now breathing short, erratic breaths on the back of my neck. I try to tell myself that we're going to be ok. Maybe once the thugs learn that they can't get anything from us, they'll leave.

"I told you already," Storm spits. "I didn't take any money from you. I was just visiting in that apartment in Victoria. There were a few of us partying and at the end of the night, then I went home. How was I supposed to know that it was your place and that you had something stolen?"

"Put them all somewhere while I think," Wolf orders Thorn.

Thorn walks past us and through the living room, disappearing into the back hall. After a few moments, he comes back and grabs Storm by the hair. Ivy and I huddle together as Thorn leads Storm to the back of the room and out of sight. Not long after we hear Storm protest and then a door slam. He reappears and walks toward Ivy and me. Thorn reaches out and grabs onto my arm. His hand is so big, my limb looks like a twig in his grasp.

"No," Ivy cries. "Please don't take her." Her hands clutch my other arm.

"Stop this, Thorn," I say desperately. "Ivy and I have nothing to do with your money. Storm showed up here in the middle of the night. Ivy and I were sleeping. We're innocent."

Wolf chimes in, "Well then, I guess you should keep better company."

It doesn't take much for Thorn to pry Ivy's hand off me. Before I know what's happening, he's half-dragging me in the same direction he took Storm. Once we round the corner to the hallway, I see a broom handle sticking through the wooden door latch on the pantry. He slides the broom out and opens the door. The light is on in the small room and Storm is crouched in a corner with her knees pulled up. After he pushes me inside, Storm grabs a tin of tomatoes and throws it at him. He laughs and slams the door.

I'm just about to say something to Storm when the door reopens, and Ivy is pushed into the pantry with us.

The room is the size of a closet. My dad always stocks it well over the winter but by the time summer rolled around, only a few items remain. Tomatoes, he always buys way too many cans of damn tomatoes.

"Are you ok, Ivy?" I take a step forward and stand beside her. She's wrapped her arms around herself and is staring at the floor. I look her up and down, hoping that Thorn didn't hurt her anywhere.

"Say something, Ivy," I say gently, touching her arm.

"Like what?" she asks, without looking up. "Like, I told you that she was toxic. I warned you. Is that what you mean by saying something?"

"Screw you, Little Miss Judgmental," Storm hisses.

"Shut up, Storm." I glare at her. "Ivy is right. You've ruined my life once and this is your second attempt at it."

The anger drains from her face, and she gives me that watery-eyed gaze. "I never meant to bring this down on you, Paisley. You don't know how sorry I am." She shakes her head hard. "But I'm telling you, I never did what those fools say I did. I've been living right. I gave up the crime and the bullshit."

"That's funny," says Ivy. "Because this room is permeated with the stench of crap right now."

"Ok," I say, holding up my hands. "Let's stop this back-and-forth bickering. It's not going to get us out of this situation. We need to put our heads together and come up with a plan."

Storm shakes her head. "You were always so naïve, Paisley. We can't sneak around these guys, or fight them. They want their money and they ain't leaving without it."

Ivy slumps with her back against the door and lets out a long, frustrated breath. For a few moments, the three of us sit in silence, until Storm speaks up again. "Maybe there is one thing that could work."

"Like?" I say, not feeling very confident with any idea she could possibly come up with.

"I don't know if it will work, but maybe it's worth a shot. These guys obviously know about me. They know that I used to do drugs and other things. So, they must know that I am connected to some pretty big players. Players with money."

"You're point?" Ivy says.

"My point is, if I can convince them to let me borrow the money that they think I owe them, I can set them up and it may give us the chance to get away."

I scoff. "I highly doubt they're going to let us walk out of here based on a promise that we'll be right back with their loot."

"They're not too bright, Paisley," Storm insists. "If I can talk to them, convince them to drive us to a place in Vancouver to get the cash, we can make an escape. At least if we're in the city, there'll be more opportunity to get away."

The room goes quiet for a minute. Then, Ivy pipes up, "How much money are we talking about anyway?"

"Fifty large," says Storm.

I feel my mouth drop open. "You can't be serious."

"I'm a hundred percent serious. They think I pinched fifty g's, yet I had to hitchhike here. See, I told you. They're not too bright."

"Let's hope you're right about that, because this plan could never work unless they are complete idiots."

Storm stands up. She brushes herself off and finger combs her hair, then puts her shoulders back and draws in a deep breath. "Wish me luck," she says, moving past us and rapping hard on the thick pantry door. Ivy and I huddle against the back wall.

We wait silently for a response, listening for the sounds of footsteps in the hall. After a long wait of nothing, Storm grabs one of the cans of tomatoes from the bottom shelf. She smiles and shows it to us. "Well, if this doesn't work, nothing will."

She bashes the tin hard in the middle of the door. The sound rips at my eardrums in the small room and sets my anxiety to the highest level. After ten or so crashes to the door, she stops and again, we wait to hear any signs of the thugs. After a minute or two, Storm looks at us, shrugs, then puts the now dented tin back on the shelf. She's just about to say something when we hear the rattling of the broom handle being dislodged from the door. A second later, Thorn is standing in the doorway, face-to-face with Storm.

"What the hell is your problem?" he says.

"I don't have a problem, dude, only a solution."

"I hope it involves a shit load of money."

"It does."

He grabs Storm by the front of the shirt and yanks her into the hallway before slamming the door. Once Ivy and I are alone, I turn to her. She looks paler than usual and her eyes are wide and she is traumatized. The more I look at her, the harder she seems to be trembling. Suddenly, I am overwhelmed by guilt. Even though I have nothing to do with Storm anymore, it's because of Storm's connection to me that this is happening and Ivy, sweet Ivy, never asked for any of it.

"I am so sorry," I say, putting a hand on her shoulder. "This is all my fault."

"How? You didn't invite her here, did you?"

"Of course not."

"Then you have nothing to be sorry for." She looks deep into my eyes. Her earlier flash of anger is gone.

"But, if I wouldn't have—"

"It doesn't matter what we did or didn't do. We're stuck in this mess now and if Storm's plan doesn't work, we've got to put our heads together and come up with a better idea." She sounds like her old logical self.

"You're right. All that matters is that we stay cool and don't let our fear get in the way."

I lean in and hug her tightly. I feel her heart racing against my chest, but her body is trembling a lot less now. Maybe she's trying to suppress her fear so she can think effectively— smart girl. As I hold her, I am flooded with protectiveness. No matter what happens, I will do my best to protect her, even if it means putting myself in danger.

I'm just about to tell her not to worry when we hear Storm holler from outside the pantry door. Ivy and I look at each other in fear.

The door opens, and Storm is standing in front of us with Wolf behind her. Her head is down and she's leaning forward. Then Wolf raises his leg and kicks her in the middle of the back, sending her crashing into Ivy and me. The door shuts and we wait until we hear the broom handle slide into place before we say anything.

"So, I guess we're on to Plan B, huh?" Ivy says darkly.

Storm doesn't raise her head.

"Well, aren't you going to tell us what happened out there?" I say, looking at her.

Slowly, Storm raises her head and reveals a cut on the top of her mouth with fresh blood seeping out of it. Surprisingly, it's Ivy who speaks out. "You're bleeding. Are you ok?"

I can't believe she's actually showing concern for the person who brought this situation on us all. I can tell by Ivy's face that she's also shocked. Looking defeated and hopeless, Storm glances at me, then Ivy. A feeling of despair fills the small room.

But then, I notice the corners of Storm's bloodied mouth go up. "Of course it worked. Why wouldn't it? It was, after all, my plan."

"What do you mean, 'It worked?'" I ask.

"I mean that the goons fell for it. Wolf is going to take me to Vancouver to get the cash. As soon as I am in the city, I'll wait for the right moment, then I'll bolt. I'll get some of my pals to find Wolf, and he'll get his ass beat to shit. Then we'll come back here and then take down Thorn and free you two—"

"Wait a minute," I interrupt. "What do you mean, *you'll* go to the city? You're not actually thinking of leaving Ivy and me here alone with one of them, are you?"

"I tried. I tried to talk them into letting you come with me, but they wouldn't go for it." She pointed at her face. "I even yelled at them. That's when they bashed me in the mouth."

"Great," says Ivy, sounding defeated again. "Paisley and I will be stuck here with one of those freaks. Who knows what he'll do to us?"

"Don't worry. I'll be back before you know it. Thorn won't have time to do anything to you. Plus, you heard them. They don't want us for anything but the money."

"When will you go?" I ask.

"Soon, I think. They're probably talking about that in the other room now."

No sooner do the words leave her lips than we hear the sound of the broom being removed from the door.

"Stay positive you guys," Storm whispers. Then she looks straight into my eyes. In them, I see the ghost of what I once loved. "I know that I've done some shitty things to you, Paisley. And I guess I understand why you've moved on. But please believe me that I do feel badly about everything. All I'm asking is that you trust me to make things right."

164

And for the first time, I believe her. Her eyes fill with tears as the door opens.

After she's gone, Ivy slips her hand into mine and squeezes. A feeling of trepidation fills the room.

* * *

We listen as Storm and Wolf leave the house. The front door slams.

"I hope she knows what she's doing," Ivy says.

"I don't think Storm has ever done anything without scheming. No matter what, she'll find a way to escape. That's what she does—wrongs people, then flees." I stare at the closed door. "The question isn't if she'll find a way to save herself. It's whether she'll save us."

I feel Ivy's eyes on me, and I turn to see that the blood has drained out of her face.

Immediately I wish I hadn't said what I did. "Don't be scared, Ivy. Everything is going to be ok. If Storm doesn't come back for us by tomorrow night, we'll figure our own way out of this mess."

"Do you promise?" she says, on the verge of tears.

"Of course I do." I grab her and hug her tightly.

* * *

We don't have our cell phones, so we have no way of knowing what time it is. Everything is quiet outside the pantry door, like nobody else is in the house. Ivy and I are sitting against the back wall, shoulder to shoulder with our hands interlocked. To keep Ivy calm and to pass the time, I talk her into playing stupid games with me, like I-Spy and Guess What Song I'm Humming.

After what feels like hours, Ivy tells me that she has to pee. The last thing I want to do is bang on the door and have Thorn come in. It's been so quiet in the rest of the house, I've been hoping he fell asleep.

Instead of pushing our luck by disturbing the goon, I try to find something in the small, cluttered room for a container that Ivy can pee in. I dig through empty cardboard boxes and old paint cans while Ivy stands behind me, doing a desperate pee dance. "I really can't hold it any longer, Paisley," she bursts out, after my search leads to nothing. "I've got to go to the washroom, I'm serious."

I exhale with apprehension and pick up a can of pork and beans. Ivy stands back as I clunk the tin against the door. It isn't long before we hear footsteps coming up the hallway. Then, the sound of the door being unlocked.

I quickly put down the tin and join Ivy at the back of the pantry. I can feel my heart rate speed up and my breathing become shallow. Thorn pulls the door open, his burly frame filling the entrance.

"Ivy has to use the—"

He cuts me off, raising a finger to point at Ivy. "You!" he says, glaring at her, as though I weren't even there. "Come here!"

Ivy and I immediately grab onto each other. *What does he want her for? What's he going to do?*

"What do you want?" Ivy says, her voice shaky and weak.

"I told you to get over here!" His eyes are dark and severe.

Ivy's body trembles as she starts to cry.

"Please, don't take her," I plead. "Take me instead."

But I know, just by looking at him, that he's on a mission. Nothing I say is going to divert him from it. "If I've got to ask you one more time," he says in a low voice, "you'll both regret it."

I glance at Ivy. She looks like a scared, vulnerable child. Her head is hanging, and tears are streaming down her face. She's never been exposed to evil, not like this. I have to protect her.

"Take me instead!" I say again.

He flashes a horrible grin as he takes a step toward us. "Don't worry, your time will come."

"If you come one step closer...I swear!" I say, my voice shaking.

Before we know it, Thorn has cleared the distance between us. He leans down, the putrid stench of alcohol blowing in our faces as he speaks. "I said, you're coming with me."

"Please, *no*," Ivy begs, just as Thorn grabs her by the hair.

I reach out and claw at his face. With his other hand he shoves me with such force that my head cracks hard against the wall. I slide to the ground, feeling like I'm going to pass out. I watch through double vision as the horrible beast drags my Ivy, kicking and screaming, out of the pantry.

Ivy's cries become faint as she's dragged down the hall. I pull myself to my feet and try to reach the door, but my equilibrium is off. I fall and my knees hit the cold cement floor.

As I lie on the pantry floor, terrible pictures flash through my mind of Thorn ripping Ivy's clothes from her shaking body. I would give anything to trade places with her. She hasn't had the same exposure to bad people that I have. The gangs in prison—how they would target the vulnerable ones. How the guards would make examples of inmates who didn't behave. The things you see in the joint do something to you. Something that changes you forever.

I never thought I could feel anything again. I was numb until Ivy crept her way into my heart.

*I have to protect her. Whatever it takes.*

# Chapter Ten

It takes a few hours before I feel strong enough to move again. I move my hands to brace against the floor, making sure not to move too quickly. I try not to get dizzy as I use all my strength to push myself onto my knees.

My head feels heavy and weird as I slowly crawl to the shelf. After grabbing a tin of tomatoes, I use the shelf to help me up. It seems to take forever, raising myself bit by bit, fighting the dizziness.

When I'm finally standing on my weak, shaky legs, I take a few long breaths before moving my feet. One hand on the wall, I creep slowly to the door.

I raise the tin of food and am just about to smash it into the door when I hear the broom being taken out of the latch.

My heart pounds and I stagger back. I feel a mix of terror and hope. He's bought her back. I watch as the door opens.

Thorn is standing in the doorway. He's alone. All the air escapes my lungs.

"Where's Ivy?" My voice is desperate and weak.

"I wouldn't worry so much about her. Worry about yourself."

When Thorn's tree stump hand grabs me, I realise just how feeble I am under his strength. He drags me by the arm down the short hallway and into the living room.

The bright light of the sun makes me squint and temporarily lose my vision. Thorn flings me hard onto the sofa. I gain my bearings and quickly scan the room. My heart sinks. Ivy isn't here.

"Where is she?" I demand.

"Somewhere quiet." He towers over me. "Do you want to see her again?"

I nod, feeling a tear run down my face.

"Then do as I say."

He slowly undoes his pants.

"Oh, God. Please don't do this."

A sneer pulls at his mouth. He doesn't say anything, he just continues removing his pants while he stares at me. I pull my knees up to my chest and wrap my arms around them.

When his pants are off, he sits on the couch beside me, then bends to remove his socks. He's wearing baggy boxer shorts with a worn waistband. My heart is pounding, and I feel like throwing up.

"Please don't do this," I say again.

Thorn laughs callously as he rolls up each sock and throws them on the chair.

"I'm gay. I'm not into guys."

"I couldn't care less."

He stands again and pulls off his shirt. His skin is olive-colored and there are large zebra stretch marks on his chest and hips. He was probably fat once and then lost the weight. His abs and pecs stick out like chiseled rock. His legs look like two giant ham hocks. I briefly close my eyes, hoping that my dizziness returns so I can feel like I'm somewhere else.

"Kneel on the floor."

"Don't do this."

His face twists with a look of hatred. He grabs a handful of my hair and pulls me to the floor.

I close my eyes and rock back and forth. I am not here. I am somewhere safe and peaceful. If I can just make my mind leave the room, I can get through this.

I hear scuffling but I'm too afraid to look. I want to scream but it's pointless. There's no one to hear me. All screaming will do is aggravate him.

The scuffling stops. I smell the putrid odor of his breath. He's close to me now, very close.

"Open your eyes," he demands.

"I can't!" I whisper, praying he'll let me keep them closed.

"Open your eyes now or I'll open them for you." Spit hits my face.

I force my eyes open. Thorn is kneeling in front of me, holding a small green bottle of olive oil from the kitchen.

"I want you to massage me."

I stare at the bottle. "Why?"

"Because I fucking said so."

"But why make me massage you if you're just going to...to take me afterwards?"

"Take you? Don't flatter yourself."

"You're not going to make me have sex with you?"

"You think you're the only one who prefers something else?"

"You're queer?" I blurt out.

He grabs a hold of my tank top and yanks me toward him. "Don't call me queer, you dike bitch. I've got no more use for you than you do for me. All I want is for Wolf to get back with our money so I can get out of this back-wood shack."

He undoes the cap from the bottle of oil and pours some into my hands. The thought of touching him repulses me, but at least it won't be as bad as what I thought he was going to make me do.

As I rub the olive oil over his shoulder, he instructs me where to massage and grunts when I hit the right places. After a few minutes, I decide to try and find out where Ivy is.

"Did you put her in the bathroom, or in one of the cabins?"

He chuckles harshly. "You're not even warm."

I wait for a few moments, not wanting to piss him off. "Is she hurt?" I finally ask.

"Are you hurt?"

"No. Not really."

"Then don't ask stupid questions."

172

"So, you aren't going to hurt us?"

He shakes his head and laughs again. "Use your head, Paisley. You're smarter than your innocent little friend. You've been inside. You tell me what's going to happen."

"I don't know what you mean."

"You've seen our faces. Think about it. If we let you go, the first thing you and your little girlfriend are going to do is run to the cops."

"No witnesses," I say, hopelessness creeping in.

"No witnesses."

"But what if we promised not to—"

"You think I'm a fucking idiot? Shut up and keep massaging or I'll knock your head off."

As I massage his back, my mind races along with my pulse. Of course they're not going to let us go. I can't believe that didn't occur to me before now. In the pantry, I was so focused on keeping Ivy calm and giving her hope, I didn't think of the gruesome reality that we're facing.

As soon as Wolf gets back—with or without Storm or the money—Ivy and I become loose ends. There's no way they're driving away and leaving us alive to identify them down the road.

Now I know every second matters. If Ivy and I are going to survive this, we've got to escape before Wolf returns.

My first step is finding where Thorn has locked Ivy. He seems like the big, dumb, brutish

173

type, but it doesn't mean he's blind to deceit and tricks. I'll have to get clever if I want him to tell me where she is.

As I massage his neck and shoulders, I casually broach the subject again: "Hey, Thorn. Do you know what's better than one person giving you a massage?"

"What?" he says, relaxed.

"Two people giving you a massage."

"Nice try, Paisley. You think I'd bring her up here just so you two can scheme up an escape plan? I'm not that stupid. Keep rubbing."

*Bring her* up *here*. That could only mean one thing: the wine cellar. The place is dark and dank and the size of a closet. I used to have nightmares about monsters living there when I was a little kid. She's probably scared to death.

"It's too bad you feel that way," I say, kneading the muscles in his lower back. My hands are aching, but I don't dare let up. "I mean, you're probably getting hungry by now and Ivy is an amazing cook. She even has her own catering business."

Thorn stays quiet for a few moments. I can tell he's thinking.

"I am hungry," he says slowly, and my heart leaps. "I asked Wolf to stop for a bite before we came here, but he wouldn't. I'm sitting here starving and he's probably somewhere stuffing his face."

"I can guarantee he's not eating anything as good as what Ivy can make."

174

He twists to look at me. "You sound pretty confident."

"I am," I lie.

"You'd better be right," he says, getting up and pulling his pants on. He gestures to the couch. "Sit."

I scramble onto the couch. He grabs his shirt from the floor and pulls it on as he heads for the back hallway.

I wait until he's out of sight, then quickly get up and walk to the front door. All my instincts tell me to open the door and disappear into the trees, to run until I reach help. I quash that thought. I know that if Thorn gets back and finds me gone, he'd be furious and take it out on Ivy.

Fighting a wave of hopelessness, I return to the sofa and flop down. A few moments later I hear the scuffling of feet in the back hall. I sit up straight. *Ivy.*

As soon as they round the corner to the living room, her eyes catch mine and for a brief moment we see deep into each other. She's seems physically ok—I see no blood or bruises on her face. But I can tell by the way her hair is stuck to her reddened cheeks that she's been crying. I stand up as Thorn leads her by the arm toward me.

"Ivy, are you ok?" I ask her quietly.

She nods, looking down.

"Alright, you're both here now." He practically throws Ivy at me, and I grab her so she doesn't fall. "Get in the kitchen and make me some food—and it better be good."

We shuffle into the next room with Thorn hot on our heels. He sits down at the table and pulls out his cell phone. Ivy and I walk to the counter and start setting up cooking utensils, our backs to him. When he starts listening to music—what sounds like angry rap—Ivy and I can finally speak to each other.

"Are you ok?" I ask again, being careful not to look at her.

"I won't be if I have to go back in the cellar. It's so musty and mouldy, I felt like I was choking. Our parents haven't opened the door to the cellar in ages." She sniffs hard.

I spare a quick glance at her. A lone tear escapes down her cheek.

I reach out and gently wipe it away, desperately wishing I could hold her. "It's going to be ok," I whisper. "I promise."

"You don't know that."

"Of course, I do. I know everything."

She chuckles weakly. "Come to think of it, you may be right."

"Why do you say that?"

"Because, as soon as this asshole eats what we make, he'll probably drop dead from food poisoning."

"You're not kidding. Just pray that he doesn't want us to eat, too."

"I can't believe you told him I can cook." She picks up a tomato from the counter and studies it with a look of desperation. "He'll find out pretty quick that you were lying."

"I had to do something. I couldn't stand to think of you locked in that dark little cellar."

She looks over at me, her eyes shining. "No matter what happens, I want you to know something—"

"Quit gabbing and start cooking!" demands Thorn, making us both jump.

"We are not gabbing," I snap back at him. "We were just discussing what to make."

Quickly, we start rummaging through the cupboards, pretending like we know what we're looking for. I find a half empty package of spaghetti and Ivy roots around in the bottom shelves, eventually coming up with a jar of alfredo sauce.

"I didn't know we had that in the cupboard," I say, impressed.

"Me neither. It was way in the back. Who knows how long it's been down there."

I take the sauce from her and read the label. "It's only a month or so out of date. Unfortunately, it's probably still safe to eat."

"There goes our plan of relegating him to the bathroom for the night," Ivy whispers.

I bite back a smile as I pull a pot from the cupboard.

After we fill the pot with water, Ivy opens the jar of alfredo and empties the contents into a mixing bowl. She quickly checks to make sure Thorn isn't watching before she discards the empty jar into the trash. When the water starts to boil, we add the pasta. I know that a monkey could prepare this meal, but I don't feel any less stressed as I watch the spaghetti swirl in the boiling water. With Ivy stirring the pot and keeping her eyes glued to the clock, I grab a couple of slices of bread and put them in the toaster. While they toast, I go to the fridge and grab a piece of raw garlic and some butter.

The pasta is done just as the toaster pops. Ivy drains the noodles while I butter the slices, then rub them up and down with the garlic—something I've seen my mother do many times.

I grab a plate and make sure it's perfectly clean while Ivy tosses the spaghetti in the mixing bowl with the sauce. I set the plate in front of Thorn, who is moving his head in rhythm to the annoying music, and he looks up as Ivy slowly slides the pasta on the plate and I put the garlic toast on top.

He smells the food then looks at me and Ivy. "Smells good. You girls hungry?" And without waiting for us to answer, he laughs and says, "Too bad!" before shoveling a huge bite of spaghetti into his mouth.

All I feel is relief that he's eating without complaint. I'm sure neither Ivy or I could swallow a bite of anything, even if he offered.

Ivy and I start on the dirty dishes while Thorn gorges, still listening to his shitty tunes.

"Ivy," I say, after a few minutes of cleaning. "I'm working on a plan, ok?"

Her eyes meet mine. I can tell that she wants to believe me. She looks vulnerable and scared.

"I made you a promise," I whisper earnestly. "We're going to be ok."

She nods, biting her lip. I know she's trying her hardest to believe me. I wink at her and force a smile.

Thorn slams his fork on the table, and the noise makes Ivy and I jump. For a horrible moment I think he's heard what I said. But he only reaches for the garlic bread before turning his attention back to his phone. We continue washing the dishes and putting them back into the cupboard, not daring to talk again.

When Thorn is finished eating, he stands up and pats his gut. "That hit the spot. Now, time to put you back in your pens."

My heart sinks, and the color drains from Ivy's face. "Please, can't we stay out just a while longer?" I ask him.

"What the hell for?" he says with a laugh. "I don't need you for anything else." He motions to the kitchen door.

Ivy and I walk slowly toward the living room. As soon as we're out of the kitchen, Ivy turns to Thorn. "What about your feet? Wouldn't it be nice if we rubbed your feet while you relax?"

Thorn stares at us for a few moments, then shrugs. "I guess my feet are kind of sore." He flops on the couch with a loud grunt. "But after you're done, you're going back."

Ivy and I kneel at his feet as he stretches out his legs, one foot toward me and one toward Ivy. When my fingers touch the skin on his huge foot, a noticeable body shiver runs up my back.

Thorn sees my reaction and cackles. "What's the matter, you don't like my feet?" He lifts his leg and presses his toes against my cheek.

I move backward and fake a smile. "No. I don't mind. They're just feet."

"Liar," he says, smiling.

He turns on his music as Ivy and I start to massage him. Once in a while, we make quick eye contact with each other. I can tell by the look on her face that she's just as disgusted as I am. I glance up at the clock on the wall. 11PM. We've been prisoners for over twenty-four hours.

I count the hours Storm and Wolf have been gone. They left very early this morning. If they caught the first ferry to Vancouver, they could arrive in the city long before noon. Depending on what stunt Storm pulls, she could be back on the island by now. If she is successful at getting away from Wolf, she and her friends could be on their way back here.

But then, there's the whole question of whether she'll actually come back to save us. Regardless of the promises she spewed before she left, I can't help but remember how she abandoned me before. How she let me take the rap for her.

Maybe she's changed, but I'm skeptical. I know her too well.

I look over at Ivy, who seems to be deep in thought as she rubs the beastly foot. I wonder what she's thinking about. My mind flashes back to when we were in the kitchen—how right before Thorn interrupted, she was trying to tell me something. I wonder what it was. Hopefully, she wasn't going to say something about us not making it out of here. I want her to hold onto hope. It's all we have right now.

"Where are you from?" Ivy suddenly blurts out.

Thorn looks surprised as he looks up from his phone. "What?"

"I was just wondering if you're an Island boy, or if you're from someplace else," Ivy stammers.

"Why the hell would I tell you anything about me? Are you stupid?"

Ivy puts her head down and continues to massage him. "I didn't mean to make you angry, Thorn. I'm sorry."

Why the hell would she ask him that? I mean, he's holding us against our will. As if he's going to divulge anything personal about himself to us. What was she thinking? I look up at him. His lips are pursed in anger. He continues to stare at Ivy.

I quickly intervene and try to take his focus away from her. "Silly Ivy. She's always so talkative. She even tries to chat up the tourists that rent our cabins during the summer. She drives people nuts sometimes." I let out a fake laugh.

Thorn looks from me to Ivy and shakes his head. "You broads are fucked. Rub my feet for a couple more minutes and then I'm putting you away."

He goes back to watching videos and I look over at Ivy. She looks back at me and winks.

I'm just glad that he didn't freak out and kick her or something. I don't get what the purpose of asking him anything would be. She couldn't have thought he would tell us where he was from.

Then, it occurs to me: maybe she asked him to see what he's planning on doing to us when this whole thing is over. If he's sure about getting rid of us, he wouldn't care what we knew. Why would he? We wouldn't be alive to tell anyone.

I continue to massage his foot as I look over at Ivy. When she looks back at me, I wink.

I look up at the clock. 11:30 PM. My hands are starting to cramp from the continuous rubbing. I briefly stop and open and close my stiffening fingers. Thorn looks down at me. "What's the matter? Are your poor little hands getting sore?"

"Not at all," I say, returning to massaging his foot.

He pulls his feet from our hands and sits up straight. "Ok, it's time to go back in your pens."

182

I watch Ivy's chest expand as her breathing quickens. I look up at Thorn. "Are you sure? I mean, what if you need a snack and you want someone to serve you?"

He leans forward. "Well then, I'll know right where to find you." He stands and stretches. "Now get up."

Ivy and I rise to our feet. Thorn stands aside so we can walk in front of him. I grab Ivy's hand to let her know that she's not alone, no matter what room she is placed in. "I'm only feet away from you, Ivy," I mutter. "I'm close by and I'm thinking about you every minute."

She doesn't answer. She just gives my hand a squeeze. Just as the three of us are about to turn down the hall, a rumbling noise comes from outside.

Thorn tells us to stay put, then walks back into the living room and up to the bay window. A few seconds later, we hear Thorn say, "What the hell is going on?"

Ivy and I walk cautiously into the living room. Thorn is still standing at the window, looking out over the driveway. He doesn't hear us as we slowly creep toward him, Ivy's hand still grasped tightly in mine.

"What the hell is he doing?" Thorn exclaims.

By now, Ivy and I are close enough to catch a glimpse of what Thorn is looking at. I recognize the dark sedan right away: Wolf's. The driver's door is open and the interior light is on. I try to find Storm, but there's no one in the passenger seat.

Wolf is at the back of the car, opening the trunk. He goes out of view. A few moments later he reappears, carrying something in a gunny sack. Whatever is in the canvas bag must be heavy because he has to set it down on the ground to close the trunk.

He bends down over the sack and undoes one end. Once the bag is open, he slowly pulls it down. I recognise the long raven hair instantly.

Before I can process what I'm seeing, Ivy cries out in horror. "It's Storm. He's killed her." I feel her hand shake, and her nails bite into my palm.

# Chapter Eleven

Thorn whirls around. "I thought I told you two bitches to stay in the hall." He points to the sofa. "Sit down."

Once Ivy and I are on the couch, we huddle as closely as possible. Thorn goes to the front door and opens it. He stands and looks out as the cool evening breeze rushes into the room. Ivy and I both fill our lungs with the new air.

"What's going on?" Thorn hollers into the darkness.

There's a faint response from Wolf, but I can't make out words.

Thorn looks back to Ivy and me, then turns to the doorway. "I can't. I've got the two bitches on the sofa."

Ivy's legs shake as she presses them against me. I put my hand on her knee. "Don't panic. No matter what happens, we've got to keep our heads about us."

She looks at me. Her lips are trembling. "I'll try my hardest." I see her clench her jaw, trying to stop shaking.

Both of us keep our eyes on the floor. I hear the sound of something being dragged into the house, then a loud thud. Ivy and I both look up. Thorn is holding the door for Wolf, who is standing in the middle of the room. On the floor in front of him is the long bag. Storm's head sticks out from the open end, the rest of her body still inside.

Ivy stares at Storm's lifeless body. I can tell by her short, loud breaths that she's having an anxiety attack. I nudge her with my elbow. "Stay calm, Ivy. Please."

"This bitch was heavy," Wolf says, catching his breath.

"Did she get the money?" Thorn's tone is eager.

"Does it look like she got the money?" snaps Wolf.

"What the hell happened?"

"When we got to Vancouver, she told me to drive to a hotel downtown. I pulled around the back of the inn. As soon as I stopped, she bolted. I knew there was no way she was getting our cash."

"And then?" asks Thorn.

"And then? I had to fucking shoot her, didn't I?"

Wolf's words hit me like a speeding train, completely shattering any control I have. My chest feels heavy and tight and my heart is beating so hard, I swear everyone can hear it. I feel disoriented and my vision narrows.

"Why did you kill her?" Thorn snaps. "Now we'll never get our cash back."

"Calm down. On the way back here, I came up with a plan."

"It better be a damn good one, or we're screwed, and all of this was for nothing."

"We won't be leaving here empty handed," Wolf says, looking across the room at Ivy and me.

"I don't think those two have any money," says Thorn.

"No. But their parents do."

The men go quiet as they stare at us.

Then, Wolf pipes up: "Put them in the pantry. I need to talk to you alone."

Wolf steps over the body and flops down in the chair across from us. Thorn walks over and stands in front of us. "Move!" he orders, pointing toward the back hallway. Ivy and I rise with shaky legs. Still clutching hands, we slowly make our way toward the pantry. I'm so terrified, I can't feel my weight as I walk across the floor. I feel like I'm floating.

After opening the pantry door, Thorn gives me a hard ram with his hand and I'm knocked into Ivy, almost causing both of us to fall. When the door is closed and we hear the broom handle slide into place, Ivy and I slink together to the back of the room, then slide to the floor.

"They killed Storm," Ivy whispers. "And if we don't come up with all of that money, they're going to kill us too." She takes a deep breath as tears roll down her cheeks.

187

"Don't think like that, Ivy." I put my arm around her. "You've got to stay positive. Keep telling yourself that we're going to get out of this."

"Storm thought she was going to get out of it. Look what happened to her."

"Ivy, that's different. Storm made mistakes, huge ones. She was always in danger because she never thought anything through before she did it. She probably made a run for it without thinking about getting caught."

"Or killed," blurts out Ivy.

"Or killed," I say, sighing.

"Now, they want the money from us. I sure as hell don't have that kind of cash and neither do you. And, no offense, but your father isn't going to transfer fifty g's to a bank account. He'll probably think you're working on some sort of a scam."

I know she's right. My dad would rather lose an arm than give me a large sum of cash. He's already convinced I'm a criminal, no matter how much I've tried to tell him that Storm set me up.

"What about your parents?" I suggest. "Is there any way you can get cash from them?"

"They said they'd put a down payment on a house for me, if I found something that I loved," she says slowly. "Though, they'd definitely think it was weird if I called them and demanded fifty thousand on such short notice. But I don't think we have a choice right now. I've got to try."

188

I put my hand on her shoulder. "I wish this could all fall on me. If only my father wasn't so resentful."

"It doesn't really matter which one of us does it, as long as it gets done," Ivy says, with fear in her eyes.

I'm about to hug her when the broom is taken out of the door. We both turn and watch as Wolf enters the pantry. He has the handgun, probably the one he used to kill Storm.

I reach out and grab Ivy's hand.

"Are you bitches ready to get us some money?"

"How do you propose we do that?" I ask.

"You're going to call your mommies and daddies and say whatever you have to, so they'll transfer fifty thousand into an account."

"What if they won't?" Ivy asks in a frightened voice.

"Then both of you will share a shallow grave with your skanky pal. Is that what you want?"

Ivy and I both shake our heads.

"Good! Then we're on the same page. Now, get your asses to the living room and let's make that phone call." He uses the gun to wave us out of the room.

\* \* \*

189

When we turn the corner into the living room, Thorn is sitting on the sofa, sloppily eating a bag of chips he's gotten from the kitchen. He shovels each handful of food into his mouth, bits falling over his shirt and landing on the cushions. I shiver at his wretchedness. Wolf leads us to the counter, where he has our cellphones placed side-by-side.

"So, who's the lucky one that's going to make the call?" he asks.

"I will," says Ivy. She reaches out and picks up her phone while Wolf scratches his head with the end of the handgun. No doubt an intimidation tactic. Ivy takes a deep breath and starts to punch numbers into the keypad.

As I watch her, guilt overwhelms me. *I am so sorry, Ivy. It's all my fault that we're in this mess and that you've been put in this horrible position.*

If only I had never helped Storm on that rainy night at the grocery store. None of this would be happening, and Ivy would be safe and living her life as she always did—in peace. *If we get out of this alive, I promise I will spend the rest of my life making all of this up to you.*

She puts the phone to her ear, her hand shaking as she looks at Wolf—and the gun. "Dad, hi," she says, mustering up a happy, carefree tone. "How are you doing? Are you having a good time down there?"

I'm impressed at how quickly she is able to switch from traumatized to 'everything is great' mode. I guess that's why she was head of the drama club in school.

"Dad, you're not going to believe this. I've found this once-in-a-lifetime opportunity. A house on Texada Island was just listed for sale. It's a 2-bedroom bungalow overlooking the beach. It even has its own wharf. It's everything that I've been looking for. The problem is, there are other people interested as well. I spoke to the realtor and they said that if I make an offer right now and it gets accepted, I'd just need a sizable deposit to secure it. I'm so excited, Dad. I just don't want to lose it."

Suddenly, Ivy is quiet while she listens to her dad speak. After a few moments, she says, "Fifty thousand."

She closes her eyes tight after the words leave her lips, no doubt anticipating her father's heart attack on the other end of the phone. Wolf and Thorn's eyes are glued on her as she awaits her father's answer. Finally, after what feels like forever, Ivy shrieks and says, "Thank you, Daddy. Thank you so much!"

Thorn and Wolf give each other a silent high-five—pricks! Then Thorn hands Ivy a piece of paper with the account info on it, which she relays over the phone. When the call is finished, she gently sets her cell back on the counter and turns to our captors. "You both make me sick."

The two men laugh, and Thorn says, "What time is he doing the transfer?"

"He said it will be done in the morning. He has to find a bank down there that's connected to his branch here in Canada."

"Now that she did what you asked, when are you planning to let us go?" I say, angrily.

"When we decide!" says Wolf.

"Take those bitches upstairs and lock them in the front bedroom," Thorn says to Wolf.

We are led upstairs to my parents' room. On the way in, I notice a new latch on the door with an open lock jiggling from it. They must have installed this while Ivy and I were in the pantry.

Once inside, Ivy flops down on the bed and looks up at me. She's just about to say something when I put my finger to my lips and motion to her to keep quiet until we know Wolf is gone. A moment later, we hear him fumbling with the lock, then the sound of his footsteps as he walks away. When I'm sure he's gone, I sit beside Ivy on the bed. "What were you going to say?"

"Just that one day, I will make them pay for this."

I nod. I could only imagine how she must feel after lying to her father on the phone and conning him for the money. "I'm so sorry you had to do that, Ivy," I say, putting my hand on her knee.

"I wouldn't feel bad for my dad. He's having a great time basking in the sun."

"Yeah, but he's about to be fifty g's poorer by morning."

"Not unless someone robs his bank," she says with a mischievous grin.

"What do you mean?" I ask, confused.

"I called Mr. Ho's in Courtenay, not my parents."

"Wait, what do you mean? Mr. Ho's, as in the Chinese Restaurant off Cliff Avenue?"

"That's the one!"

"I'm confused." I say, staring at her.

"Not half as confused as Mr. Ho was."

"Ivy. You didn't call the States?"

"Nope. I sure didn't."

"But if the money isn't there by morning and Wolf and Thorn find out—"

Suddenly, we hear a faint voice coming from under the bed. Both of us stop talking and look at each other. Ivy mouths the words, *'What was that?'*

We quietly get off the bed and peer underneath. The closer we get to the floor, the clearer the voice becomes. Ivy points to the vent near the wall at the head of the bed. We inch our way under the frame until we're right over the dusty vent. Again, we hear the voice, "Everything is going great. By morning, we'll have our cash and we'll be on our way back to Victoria." It's Thorn.

"Good, I hate this place. I've never been into the whole rustic camping thing. What about the two bitches? What are we going to do with them?"

"We're going to stick to the plan," says Thorn.

193

"I guess we'd better dig a couple of holes, then," Wolf says.

"Wait 'til morning. It's pitch black out there."

My heart quickens as I look over at Ivy. I can see by her eyes how terrified she is. I tap her on the shoulder and motion for her to crawl out from under the bed. Just as we're inching backwards, we hear the noise from the TV through the vent.

Once we're back on the bed, I put my around her and press my lips to her ear. Quietly I tell her that it's going to be ok.

"It's *not* going to be ok, Paisley," Ivy says bitterly. "Stop saying that. You heard them. They plan on offing us. They're ruthless. Our only hope is climbing out the window."

"We're two stories up," I say emphatically. "The front of the house is straight down. We'd break our necks."

"I'd rather die on the ground and be free than die by the hands of one of those freaks."

As awful as her words sound, I feel the same. I get up and walk over to the window, staring out into the black night. Unlatching the small window, I push on the fame until a burst of cool air rushes into the room.

Ivy walks up and stands next to me. "We've got to try, Paisley. It's the only chance we have."

I nod, filled with trepidation over what she's suggesting. "Let me think."

Ivy nods and we walk back over to the bed. As we sit together, Ivy twirls her fingers in the holes of the knitted bedspread, her eyes serious and focused. I know I should be thinking about how to escape, but oddly, my mind keeps flashing back to when I was in the ocean, the Killer Whales twisting and turning all around me. They were so happy and free.

I sigh deeply and drop my head. Then, as if she's had some big epiphany, Ivy gasps and blurts out, "I think I know what we can do."

"What do you mean?"

She pulls at the knitted blanket under us. "We can gather up all the bedsheets and whatever else is in the room, then tie them together and use them as a rope."

I hate to cast doubt over her plan, but the whole idea seems a little like a scene from an action movie and nothing that could actually work in reality. "But what if the fabric isn't strong enough to hold our weight? Or one of the knots comes undone? We'll fall two stories down."

Ivy crosses her arms. "Well, if you've got a better plan, I'd love to hear it!"

The truth is, I don't. And as ridiculous as her plan seems, it's probably the only option to get our freedom.

"You know what? It's a good plan. I'm sorry I questioned you." I force a grin.

We start with the bedsheets, tying them together first. Next, we secure the knit bed covering to the end of the sheets. Then Ivy rummages through the closet while I sift through the chest of drawers. We pile our finds on the now bare bed: large, long sweaters, a few pairs of my father's jeans, an old shawl, and a ratty old scarf. We quickly lay the garments on the floor and, one-by-one, we tie each piece to the end of our rapidly growing chain.

"I just hope all of these knots hold." I say, giving an extra yank on each tie.

"It's a good thing we're on the thin side," Ivy says.

"Yeah, I guess we can attribute that to our bad cooking skills."

Ivy lets out a little giggle and loses her balance as she's tying a cardigan to the chain. She bumps into the bedside table and I see the lamp teeter.

"No," I cry, reaching for the lamp, but it's too late.

With a thunderous crash, the bulbous lamp smashes on the floor.

"Oh crap," Ivy says, turning around to see the damage.

"That was so loud," I say, moving toward the mess to clean it up. "I hope they didn't hear that from downstairs.

We start gathering up the bigger pieces of the ceramic lamp base first, stacking the shards in little piles. Just as I'm about to pick up the lampshade and shake it off, we hear the rattling of the lock on the door.

Ivy and I jump to our feet. Ivy quickly stuffs our tied fabric under the bed and we stand in front of it. My heart is thumping so hard, it feels like it's going to burst out of my chest. Thorn swings open the door and looks around the room. "What the hell was that noise?" he barks.

At first, neither one of us knows what to say, but then I remember how Ivy had to fake the phone call downstairs. I owe it to her to take the lead now. "I accidentally knocked over the lamp," I say, looking down at the small heaps of ceramic on the floor.

His eyes follow mine to the broken lamp. "If I hear one more sound out of this room, I'm going to make you wish you were never born. Do you got that?"

We both nod obediently.

He stares into our faces as he slowly closes the door. Then, just when we think he's going to leave, he opens the door again and says, "Where the hell are the blankets?"

Ivy quickly steps forward. "It's too hot in here. We put them in the closet."

"Weird chicks," Thorn says, before pulling the door closed.

Ivy and I don't move until we hear the latch lock. Once we know he's gone, we both exhale and look at each other.

"That was close," she says.

I nod as Ivy pulls the fabric onto the mattress.

The real task is finding a secure place to fix our makeshift rope to. If we tie it to the aluminum bed leg, the leg could bend and break and make noise. Finally, we agree to use the heavy leg on the wooden chest of drawers. My mother was gifted the solid piece of furniture by her father, a furniture maker from England. Whenever we had to move the large monstrosity, she always said, "They sure don't make them like this anymore." It was this piece of furniture that always made me feel sorry for movers.

Once the cloth snake is tied and reinforced, Ivy and I use all our strength to slowly and quietly push the dresser against the wall beside the window. That way, it won't be able to move under our weight and create a huge noise, alerting the brutes downstairs.

Bit by bit, we lower the fabric out the small window. When we run out of homemade rope, it stops about six to eight feet above the ground.

"Oh no," says Ivy. "It doesn't touch the ground."

"It'll be fine. When we reach the end, we'll just have to jump. It's not that far. We can make it." I think back to when I dangled from the windowsill at Jasper's, and how Ivy had to help me down. This feels like a cruel repeat of that afternoon. What had been funny before is now making me feel sick.

Ivy swallows hard and watches as the long strand catches a gust of wind and swings back and forth. "Who is going to go first?"

She looks nervous and skeptical, so I muster all of the fake bravery I can. "I'll do it. It's a breeze," I say, winking at her. Meanwhile, my insides are churning at the thought. I've never been big on heights, but now's not the time to dwell on that. I've got to forge ahead and show Ivy that it can be done.

I slide off my shoes and tell her to do the same. "When we jump from the bottom of the rope, it might be quieter when we hit the ground. Bare feet are quieter."

Reluctantly, she sits on the bed and unties each of her trainers before sliding them off. Then, she looks up at me. "I know this was my idea, but now I'm not so sure."

"Just don't think about it, ok?" I say. "Instead, think about the house you want to live in on Texada. Think about the wonderful times we can have if we make it out of here."

Ivy puts her face in her hands and quickly rocks back and forth. After a few moments, she takes a deep breath, and says, "Ok. you're right. Let's do it!"

"Good girl! We're going to be fine. You'll see."

She holds the small window open as I grunt and groan, sliding my legs out. I feel the outside of the building and grab onto the rope, my stomach scraping across the frame. "Ouch. Grab a t-shirt from one of the drawers and lay it across the sill when you come out, Ivy. Otherwise, it'll hurt like hell."

She grimaces and holds onto the rope as I let go of the sill, my weight fully supported by the sheets. Ivy leans out of the window and watches as I slowly descend, using my feet to guide me down the wall. I keep my eyes fixated on her. The only time I look down is when she gives me two thumbs up. There's no more rope between me and what looks to be about seven feet from the ground.

I clench my teeth, look up at Ivy, and let go. I land hard, with my knees just missing my chin. Standing up quickly, I brush myself off and look up at Ivy, her blond hair illuminated by the light behind her. I wave my arms, urging her to climb down. I can tell that she's hesitating. The large bay window to the living room is about ten feet away and I can hear the men laughing at something playing on the TV. I'm too close to them. If I call out to Ivy, they may hear me. I can't take that chance. I use both of my arms and motion at her again.

Slowly, she backs away from the window and disappears.

No. What's happened? Did her fear get the best of her? Did someone enter the room? My pulse quickens and a clenching feeling forms in the pit of my gut. I have no idea what to do. I can't reach the bottom of the rope, it's too far up. Water wells in my eyes and spills down my cheeks.

Then, I see something moving in the window, something small. I keep staring until I recognize the 'thing' as Ivy's feet. A wave of exhilaration runs through me. She's doing it. She's really doing it. Way to go, Ivy.

I watch as she maneuvers out of the window and her feet find the wall. When she lets go of the frame and is suspended on the rope, I breathe a huge sigh of relief. Soon, she'll be on the ground beside me and then we'll be running like hell to get help. These bastards are going to pay for what they've done to us, and especially what they've done to Storm. No matter how many shitty things she did in her life, no one deserves to die the way she did.

Ivy is just over halfway down when I see something dangling from around her neck. At first it looks like clothing blowing in the wind, but as she gets closer, I can see that she has tied her trainers together and hung them around her neck. I feel a mixture of impressed at her foresight and dismay that she hadn't thought to grab mine.

There's only three feet or so before she'll reach the end of the rope. With each passing second, I become more filled with anticipation. I can't wait until we're away from here and out of danger.

Then, it happens. Like a scene in a horror movie, one of the knots from far above her gives way, and just like that, Ivy is plummeting from ten feet up. I try to gauge where she's going to land and position myself accordingly, but before I know it, she's lying on the ground and writhing in pain.

I freeze, not knowing what to do. Did she hurt her spine? Break a leg? She groans loudly, causing me to snap out of it.

Leaning down, I whisper loudly in her ear, "Where does it hurt?"

"My foot," she gasps.

Then, to make matters worse, the TV in the living room is silenced. My first thought is that they've heard Ivy and are heading upstairs only to find that we're not there.

I've got no choice. I tell Ivy to hold her breath, and I use all my strength to stand her up and put one of her arms around my shoulders. As we walk to the other side of the lot, toward the rental cabins, I keep looking back to the bay window to see if the front door has opened. So far, it hasn't.

By her labored breathing, I can tell that Ivy's in a lot of pain. I set her down by the cabin nearest the woods.

"What's wrong?"

"I think I broke a bone in my foot," she pants, grimacing.

"I'm so sorry, Ivy. I'll help you get out of here, every step of the way. But we have to walk."

"I'll try, Paisley. I'll go as far as I can."

"Try isn't an option. We're out of the house. We're free. Now all we have to do is walk through the woods and make it to the back road. Once we're there, it's only a mile or so to the first house. There, we can call for help. But you've got to stay strong, Ivy."

She nods, and I help her stand. I wrap her arm around my neck, and we resume walking in the direction of the forest.

"How are we supposed to make it through the bushes and trees?" Ivy points out. "There aren't even any trails back here."

"I know, but if we walk along the road, Thorn and Wolf will easily find us. The only thing we have going for us right now is that we know the area, and they don't."

# Chapter Twelve

As soon as we reach the pathway that leads to Jasper's cabin, I turn and look over at the main house. The living room light is still on and the reflection from the TV is shining on the wall. I see one pair of legs up on the coffee table. Even though I can't detect signs of someone else in the room, they must not yet know we're missing if one is still watching TV. I sigh with relief, then set Ivy down on a stump. We haven't walked far, but I can tell by the sweat beading on her face that the pain is increasing.

"I can't do it, Paisley. It hurts too much."

"You have to, Ivy. If they find us, they'll kill us."

She whimpers as I remove the trainers from around her neck and undo the laces. Maybe if I tie her shoes on really tight, it'll offer her some support. After I put the shoe on her good foot, I carefully open the second one as wide as possible and gingerly lift her bad foot. But as soon as I look closely, I see how bad the foot is swelling. There's no way it's going to fit in the shoe.

"You wear that one," Ivy says weakly.

It's probably not a bad idea. The forest floor is carpeted with all sorts of sharp vines, thistles, and roots. Not to mention that we're walking in the dark.

With each minute we wait for Ivy to rest, anxiety grows stronger in me—it's only a matter of time before they notice we're gone.

"Ivy, we've got to keep moving."

"It hurts so badly," she says, sounding defeated.

"I know, sweetie, but trust me, it's nothing like the pain Thorn and Wolf will inflict if they catch us."

As I help her stand, she moans in agony. I feel terrible. I wish there was something I could give her to help with the pain, but the aspirin is back at the house. Then, something occurs to me as we trudge up the narrow path—Jasper's cabin. I'm sure he has some kind of pain pills—he has to. I tell Ivy my idea, and with that in mind, she hops a little faster.

It seems to take forever to reach the rickety shack. By the time I set Ivy on the stairs, my shoulder feels like it's been hit with a bat. She's small, but with her foot badly injured, she's dead weight. I tell her to sit tight as I quickly climb the stairs to the door. I reach down and turn the handle, but of course it's locked. I don't know why I was expecting any different.

I carefully walk back down the stairs to Ivy. She's rocking back and forth to help sooth the pain. "I don't know how much longer I can stand this," she says, tears rolling down her cheeks.

I can tell that she's exhausted and getting close to the point where she won't be able to stand again. I've got to do something fast. I scan the ground, straining my eyes in the darkness until I see a stone about the size of a soup bowl. I quickly walk over, pick it up, then climb the stairs back to the door. It only takes a few hard whacks on the handle before I hear something break in the lock and the door swings open.

I bolt inside. It's pitch black, and I have to feel my way down the short wall to the back of the shack. When I come to a door, I push it open, praying that I've located the bathroom. My heart leaps as my hand feels the porcelain edge of a sink. Then, I feel along the wall for a cabinet. My hand hits something cool and smooth—a mirror. I pull on the edge and feel it swing open.

I rummage around, feeling the shape of a toothbrush, a comb and then, finally, a small plastic bottle that rattles—pills.

On my way out of the shack, my eyes catch something from the small bit of moonlight coming in the window. I carefully walk toward the shining object. The old wooden boards creak under my feet. When I reach the small table where the shimmering object is, I reach out my hand to investigate. My fingers run down the cool bulbous metal. It's an oil lamp.

I lift up the lamp and give it a little shake. I hear sloshing inside. Running my hands over the cluttered little table, I find a small package of wooden matches. Quickly, I sit down on the floor and light the wick.

I don't dare place the unit back on the table. Someone could see the light. I've got to keep the lamp out of sight and the flame set low. In the tiny amount of light coming from the lantern, I am able to make out the tiny kitchen. I walk over to the sink, find a small tin cup in the cupboard, and fill it with tap water.

The moment I'm through the door, I notice that Ivy is no longer rocking. Instead, she's lying back on one of the steps. A wave of panic hits me, and I throw the cup behind me as I run down the steps and kneel at her side.

"Ivy. Are you ok?" My voice cracks.

I move her so she's resting in my arms. I feel her warm breath on my neck as she moans. There's no way I can make her continue like this. I've got to get her into the cabin so she can rest properly for a while. I try to help her stand, but unlike before, she's putting no effort into helping. There's no way she's going to be able to hop up any of these steps. I help her balance, and then I bend down, flop her over my shoulder and lumber up the stairs.

By the time we're in the cabin, I'm dizzy from not being able to breath under her weight. As carefully as I can, I flop her onto a spindly chair beside the table. She folds her arms on the table and rests her head on them.

I locate the tin cup and rinse it in the sink before refilling it with water. I pull the pill bottle from my pocket and hold it close to the lamp. In small black letters are the words, Extra-strength Aspirin. I shake out two large white tablets. "Ivy," I say, jiggling her shoulder. "Take these pills, honey. They'll help with the pain."

She looks up at me, her eyes glassy and red. "Thank you," she says. A tear rolls down her cheek.

As I stare back at her, I feel as though there's a vice around my heart, squeezing until it's just about to break. I wish I could take her pain away. When I give her the tin cup to wash down the pills, I notice how hard she's shaking. It becomes apparent very quickly—walking through the woods with her is going to be near impossible. She has no support for her bad foot, even with my help. After she swallows the last pill, I make sure she's steady on the chair before I start rummaging through the shack.

There's a small baker's shelf with two wooden doors. It looks like it was built a century ago. When I pull one of the doors open, the motion stirs up a bunch of dust and I hack and sneeze. All I see is more dust and tons of small brown pellets—mouse shit. Next, I cross the room to what looks to be a tall broom closet. Holding my breath, I slowly open the door. There's nothing but an old-fashioned broom and a few pairs of tattered footwear. I grab an old boot with holes in the toe and then a slip-on loafer. I look over at Ivy, then back to the slipper in my hand. If I can find a towel or something else to pad it, I can makeshift a soft cast around the loafer.

For the next few minutes, I gather what I can from under the sink, in the drawers and off a rack in the bathroom. Just as I'm about to head back to Ivy, I spot something on the bathroom counter. I smile as I pick up the scraper.

With a roll of duct tape, the slipper, and a few rags, I sit on the floor next to Ivy and slowly move her foot toward me. She groans loudly but doesn't pull away.

"I'm just going to make you a little brace, ok?"

She lifts her head and nods. Her eyes are looking a little more clear. The pills must be starting to work. I pull the lamp closer so I can get a better look. As soon as the dull light shines onto her foot, the severity of her injury becomes apparent. Her entire foot is puffy and starting to turn black with bruises. There is no definition to where her ankle would normally be, there's just swelling all over.

"Is it bad?" she asks, her voice sounding a little stronger.

"No, silly. It's not bad at all. You've probably just sprained it."

She giggles a little and shakes her head. "You're a bad liar, Paisley."

I smile warmly. "You're going to be just fine."

As I work on her foot, she reaches down and caresses my arm. "Thank you."

209

"Do you mean, thank you for urging you to jump out of a window?"

"It's not your fault, Paisley. It was my idea. Plus, we had no other option. The window was the only way out."

"Well, I guess we can add something else to the list of things we can't do besides cooking."

"What's that?"

"We make shitty Spiderwomen."

She smiles. "True that."

A couple of times she has to hold her breath while I continue wrapping her foot. When I'm finished, she lets out a huge sigh. "That actually feels better. I mean, it still throbs like a bastard, but the sharp pains are easing."

I smile and hug her. My brave Ivy. I just hope that now we can get out of here before the two thugs find us. Surely by now one of them has gone upstairs and noticed we're gone.

I get another cup of water for Ivy, then drink one myself. If we're going to be trudging through the woods for a long time, we'll need to be hydrated.

"Do you think you can try again?" I ask.

"Yeah. I'll give it my best shot. I just hope I don't slow you down too much."

"Either way, I'm not leaving you."

She smiles up at me, then braces her arms on the table to help her stand. I gently grab one of her arms and lift. Once she's on her feet, we slowly shuffle across the dusty floor toward the door. She's not as wobbly as she was without the makeshift wrap. Hopefully, the pain won't be as awful when the aspirin wears off. *The Aspirin, I'd better take the bottle with us.* I prop Ivy against the door and go back to the table and retrieve the small bottle.

We stand for a moment at the top of the stairs, looking out into the unwelcoming night, the tall trees staring down at us. We are alone, half of us broken and the other half unsure. Taking a deep breath, I muster my courage as I take the first step down, guiding Ivy to the stairs, securing her weight with my arm. I'm just about to help her down the step when Ivy gasps. "Did you hear that?" she says.

"Hear what?"

"There's something out there."

"I don't hear anything. It's probably just the wind."

Her voice lowers to a faint whisper. "Stop. Listen. You'll hear it."

Impatient to get down the stairs, I huff and briefly stop moving. With my eyes on Ivy, who is staring off to the pathway, I listen.

A long moment passes and I'm just about to resume walking when I hear a scuffing noise coming from the narrow dirt lane.

A cold shiver runs over me. The sound wasn't from an animal. Animals either take slow, crunching steps in the thicket, or quick short ones on the dirt. A strong feeling of impending doom rushes over me and I step up to the same stair where Ivy is.

"Someone is coming," she says with finality.

"I'm sure it's just a coyote or a small creature, Ivy. But let's go back inside until it passes by." I know I'm lying, and that she's right—someone is approaching in the darkness. But I need to sound calm and in control, if not for Ivy, then for me. We can't afford to panic.

I quickly help Ivy back into the shack, shutting the door softly behind us. As we stand against the wall in the eerie orange hue of the dying lantern flame, we hear the unmistakable sound of wood creaking from weight on a step. And then, everything goes silent.

"They're here," Ivy breathes.

I quickly scan the room for something to defend ourselves with. There's a short, thin bar beside the small fireplace on the other side of the room, but when I go to move, Ivy grabs onto me tighter.

Another creak echoes through the room. Our bodies are trembling so hard, I can hear Ivy's teeth chattering.

I wrap my free arm around her in a weak attempt at shielding her from whoever is about to enter. It doesn't matter if it's Thorn or Wolf—they have a gun, therefore, they have all the power. They decide our fate.

The noise is deafening as they step on the final stair. Our fear has taken all the oxygen out of the room, making it hard to breath. We watch as the knob on the door turns. Ivy's knees buckle and she slides against the wall to the floor. Still standing, I step in front of her. Slowly, the door creaks open. My chest heaves as I gasp for air. Ivy wraps her arms around my legs, and I feel the tiniest burst of courage. *Whatever it takes.* I straighten my back and put my chin up.

I see a rugged boot appear, then another. His face is hidden in the shadows. He stands in the doorway, huge.

Ivy bursts into a fit of sobbing. I put my hand on her head. The floor creaks as the man steps into the cabin. I see the rugged long jacket and baggy worn jeans. Then the weak light of the lantern hits his face, and the craggy lines on his forehead.

My legs finally give way and I land on my knees beside Ivy. A sob of relief chokes me.

"What the hell are you two doing in my place?"

At the sound of his voice, Ivy looks up through her tears. "Jasper?"

"I asked you a damn question. What business do you have here?"

I cover my face with my hands and my sobs turn to laughter. "Jasper, how did you get here?"

"How the hell do you think I got here? I drove. I only made it as far as Merville Store before I ran out of—wait a minute. You never answered my question. What are you two doing in here?"

"Running for our lives," Ivy cries.

Jasper looks at me. "What the heck is she going on about? Have you two been drinking?"

"No. There are two men at the house. They're armed and they killed Storm. They're probably looking for us right now. Didn't you see their car parked in the lot?"

"There was no car in the driveway besides yours," he says. "I just walked past the house. Ain't no men that I saw. The whole house was dark. Listen, you've probably been into something that's messed with your minds—"

Ivy grabs onto one of his legs, and Jasper stares at her in shock. "Jasper, please listen to her. She's telling you the truth. There are two brutes that had us locked in the upstairs bedroom. They had me call my dad and ask for fifty thousand dollars. Then we overheard them say that after they get the money, they're going to kill us. The car's probably not there because they're out looking for us."

Jasper is listening to Ivy in a way he didn't listen to me. For a few long moments, he says nothing. "What happened to your foot?" he finally asks.

"We escaped out of the room on the second floor. While we were shimmying down a rope we made, I fell. I think it's broken."

He looks perplexed as he tries to make sense of what we've told him.

"Please, Jasper," I say. "Please help us. Ivy needs a doctor badly."

He looks at me. Then he seems to make up his mind. "As I said, my truck ran out of gas just past the store. I've got a jerry-can with enough fuel to get to town, but it'll be some time before I get back here."

"No, don't leave us here alone, Jasper. Please!" cries Ivy.

I crouch down beside her. "He has to get the truck, Ivy. Then we'll get out of here." I look up at Jasper, "I don't know how you got past the house undetected. Please, be careful when you leave. They're dangerous."

He scoffs. "No offense, but you are two young women with everything to lose. I am an old man. I've done most of my living. I don't fear easily, especially because of a few worthless punks."

"Just be careful," I add, before unwrapping Ivy's arms from his legs.

She puts her hands around my neck, and we stand. To mine—and Jasper's—surprise, Ivy hugs him, and he coughs and leaves the cabin.

I follow him to the door and watch him move a couple of boards in front of the house before pulling out a red plastic Jerry-can. "Remember, they're armed," I whisper loudly.

He nods and I watch as he starts down the path. It isn't long before the darkness swallows him up.

I close the door behind me. Ivy is now sitting at the table, tapping her fingers on her leg. "Do you think he'll make it past them?"

"I'm sure he will. He got here safely, didn't he?" I try to sound upbeat while my insides churn. "How is the pain, Ivy?"

"Suddenly, it's getting a lot worse."

I pick up the cup and fill it with water before shaking out two more pills from the bottle and handing them to her. After she's taken them, I carry the flickering lamp to a tiny back room—about the size of the pantry in the main house. A single cot sits beneath a little window. Ivy will be a lot more comfortable in here, and she'll be able to rest her foot until Jasper gets back.

Once Ivy is on the bed, she lets out a long breath. I place the lamp on the floor and sit beside her, slowly stroking her hair.

She looks up at me and the corners of her mouth rise. "Everything is going to be ok, right?"

"Right. Just focus on that perfect little house on Texada."

"Yeah," she says, sounding like she's starting to relax.

"It will be bright, safe and beautiful."

"And you'll be there with me," she says, closing her eyes.

"Definitely," I whisper.

After a few minutes, I can hear her breathing lengthen. She's sleeping, I'm not sure if she passed out so quickly because of the exhaustion from a night of trauma, or if the pills are kicking in, but I'm just grateful she's relaxed enough to sleep.

I slowly lean over and grab the lamp, then gently stand and tiptoe into the front room. I peer out of the dirty front window and don't see a thing. Then I open the front door and step out onto the narrow stair. It will be a while before

Jasper makes it back. I go back inside and take a seat at the small table.

In my head I go over the distance between here and the Merville store. It's a dark night, and even though he knows the area better than anyone, there are always surprises. Black bears and their young cubs are common to the area, as are cougars and timber wolves. Even though I'm confident that Jasper knows how to scare off lurking wildlife, meeting with an unexpected creature could waste precious time. I just hope that after he makes his way to his truck, he'll find a helpful local to let him use their phone. If I know Jasper, he won't wait for the authorities to arrive. Instead, he'll make his way back here to rescue Ivy and me.

* * *

The boom of the gunshot shakes the windows in the small cabin and sends a wave of terror through me.

I jump to my feet. My legs are shaking so violently that my knees are knocking into each other. I've got to get Ivy out of here.

When I get to the room, Ivy is already sitting up in the bed. "What was that?"

"I need you to come with me," I say, unable to hide the trembling in my voice.

"They've killed him, haven't they?"

"I don't know, Ivy. All I know is that I heard a loud bang, and we can't take the chance that he's not coming back. We've got to get out of here right now."

She stands, wobbling, and I wrap her arm around my neck. As quickly as possible, I walk her to the front door as she hops to keep up.

Just as we're about to walk out, we see a light shining through the trees.

"They know that we're up here," Ivy says, starting to hyperventilate.

It's coming from a way down the path. If we move quickly, we'll make it into the cover of the forest before they get to us.

"We don't know who it is, Ivy. It could even be Jasper."

"Yeah, right, Paisley. It's a little hard to hike up here if you've got a bullet hole in you."

"We're not positive someone did get shot. Maybe Jasper made it past them, and they were just goofing around with the gun."

"Hardly," she says, putting weight on my shoulder as she takes her first step down.

I take another step before lowering her down. Every once and awhile, we look over to the base of the path and see the light getting a little brighter—they're getting closer. With Ivy's arm around me, I try my hardest not to shake. If she feels my nervousness, hers will amp up, too.

When we're two steps from the bottom, I get in front of her and tell her to get on my back. We are out in the open and I need to get us into the woods, now.

The weight of her pushes my feet into the dirt. As I trudge toward the trees, my legs feel weak and unstable—I feel like I'm walking in deep sand. Every step takes all my strength. The trees get closer. So does the light.

The moment we pass the edge of the woods, the light and whoever is behind it reaches the top of the path. Ivy climbs off my back and we slowly make our way deeper into the dense forest.

I use the trees as a guide while I lead Ivy over the forest floor. As soon as the glow from the flashlight is out of view, I can barely see my feet. I secure each step I take so Ivy can follow in my footsteps. As she limps behind me, I hear soft groans and gasps whenever she steps down on her hurt foot. I quietly whisper that she is doing great—we've just got to keep moving.

* * *

The dim glow from the night sky offers little light on the forest floor. Still, the stars are bright and even though the canopy above is thick, I can make out the Big Dipper in the breaks. When I was a little girl, my dad would wake me up, wrap me in my blanket and, while my mother slept, he would take me to the beach and point out the stars. The Big Dipper was always my favorite because it was the easiest to see. From there, I could find the Little Dipper and Cassiopeia.

I smile and feel a warmth pass through me at the memory. I wish I were young again. I felt so safe wrapped in my blanket, sitting beside my dad.

I feel resistance in my hand as Ivy lags. I turn to her. "What is it?"

"I'm dizzy. I can't walk anymore. Just leave me here. I'll wait while you go for help."

"I can't leave you by yourself. It's only a matter of time before the goons catch up. We've got to keep moving."

"No, Paisley. I'm done. I'm telling you. I can't do it anymore. I'm going to pass out. It hurts too much."

I can tell by her tone that no amount of me trying to encourage or convince her is going to change her mind. It becomes painfully clear that the only way we're getting out of here together is if I carry her. The ground is uneven and full of protruding roots—I won't get far with her on my back. But I know I have to try.

We rest for a few long minutes before I convince her to let me pack her. After a few failed attempts, Ivy is finally slumped on my back and I'm slowly moving forward. After accidentally knocking her foot as I tried to maneuver between two trees, she becomes weaker—and heavier. My legs cramp and my breathing becomes laboured as the ground passes slowly under my feet.

After some time, I see a small clearing ahead, and cautiously maneuver my way there. Finally, I can set her down and catch my breath.

When we're sitting side by side and our breathing slows, I hear something in the distance—trickling and stirring. It's the small stream that runs parallel to our property. If we can reach it, all we have to do is follow it upstream and it will lead us close to the road. Finally, some good luck.

Ivy flops her head onto my shoulder. I stroke her hair as she pants in pain. "We have to get up and walk again soon."

She doesn't answer me. Instead, she starts to sob. My first instinct is to persuade her, as I've been doing all along, but this time, I know she's done.

If I have any chance of saving her, I'm going to have to get help on my own.

"Sorry," she says, weakly.

"Don't be. You did so well. I'm so proud of you. You have nothing to apologize for."

When she looks up at me, there are tears streaming down her dirty face. I'm scared to leave her, but I have no choice. The terrain is too difficult for her and the trees are so close together, I'd never make it through with her on my back.

Still, I can't leave her vulnerable and out in the open. I have to make sure that she's well hidden until I come back.

Across from where we're sitting is a large rock covered in moss. If I can lay her on her side and pull the moss from the stone, I might be able to conceal her. Plus, the rock will serve as a landmark so I can easily find her again.

221

"Ivy, I'm not going to make you walk anymore, ok? Do you want to stay here while I run to get help?"

I feel her nod as I gently stroke her hair.

"But you've got to lie behind that big rock over there, so that you're out of sight. Ok?"

"I want to lie down. I'm so tired," she whispers, her voice barely audible.

I make sure she's secure before I get up and start peeling small sheets of moss from the rock. Once I'm finished, I stomp on the earth and make sure it's level. I help Ivy move behind the rock, lowering her down onto her side. Kissing her forehead, I put my lips to her ear. "Don't worry my beautiful Ivy. I'll be back as soon as I can."

After covering her with the moss and some nearby dead branches, I'm just about to leave when Ivy moans something. I lean down as closely as I can. "What did you say?"

"I love you."

I can't move and suddenly, the darkness lifts and I'm standing in a warm glow of light. She loves me.

I reach down and touch her face with the back of my hand. "I love you too, my Ivy."

# Chapter Thirteen

As I navigate around every size of tree with spikey stems and spindly branches scraping into my flesh, I think about the three words she said. *I love you.* But how can she love me? I'm the one that got her into this mess. It's my fault that she's lying on the cold, dirty ground, covered with moss. And it's even my fault that she got injured. Without me around, she wouldn't have needed to escape from anyone. My heart weighs with guilt and my eyes fill with tears, making it even harder to see as I walk through dark forest.

Picturing her lying behind the big rock, cold and alone, I pick up my pace, using my hands to help navigate obstacles in front of me. Soon, the sound of the stream grows louder, and I know I must be getting close. I fall a couple of times on slippery roots. Warm blood trickles down my knees and one of my elbows. I know the pain is nothing compared to what Ivy is feeling, so I suck it up and keep moving. Then, the ground starts to slope down, and before I know it my one foot—the bare one—is standing in the cold, flowing water of the stream.

I crouch down, cup my hands, and take a long drink of fresh water. I quickly rinse off my wounds and splash water on my face. And just as I stand up, a shrill scream travels through the trees like an eerie scene in a horror movie. A second later it repeats, louder.

The only thing I can think is, *I have to reach her in time.*

I'm moving so quickly, I can't feel the pain from the branches and sharp sticks as they pierce my skin. All my senses are focused on rescuing her. My lungs burn for a rest, but I know if I take even a second to stop, it could mean the end.

Up ahead, my eyes catch a glimpse of bright flashes bouncing between the trees. As I get closer, I hear voices. High voices. Not the voices of Thorn or Wolf.

Then, Ivy screams again. Her agonized cries make me want to scream to her that I'm coming, but if I do, it will take away the only thing I have going for me— the element of surprise.

Whoever is hurting her could have weapons. The only chance I have is to sneak up on them in the darkness and hope that they don't spot me in the beam of their flashlight.

I can hear their voices a lot plainer now. And in between Ivy's cries, I make out words from her captors.

"Does that hurt, Princess?" The voice is sadistic and strong.

The beam of light is pointing downward at the rock where I left Ivy. She screams and I use the noise to step closer undetected. Again, I hear the voice of the same woman: "You girls weren't going to run away before we got our money, were you?"

I'm close enough to see Ivy. They have her sitting against the rock. Her bandaged leg is splayed out while the other is pulled up to her chest.

I watch as a slender figure crouches down and grabs her by the hair. "Where is that little bitch? Is she hiding somewhere around here?"

My heart skips a beat and I freeze. The voice of Ivy's attacker. I know it.

I force myself to draw in a breath as my brain struggles to comprehend what I'm hearing and seeing. As I watch the dark silhouette of the willowy woman, I recognize her body movements and the tone of her voice.

Storm.

I don't understand. She was dead. Ivy and I both saw her lifeless body in the canvas bag at the house.

Then, the second woman interrupts. "Give me the flashlight. I'll look around for the other skank." As soon as I hear Storm's accomplice, my mind flashes back to jail and the intimidating rasp of the cell block terrorizer—Violet.

Storm shines the light on her. She looks different than she did in prison. Now, she has dark, shoulder-length hair and bright lipstick that glows in the light. My mind immediately goes back to the other day when Ivy and I were shopping, and I put the cart back. That woman, the one in the red compact car, the one that was staring at me. I couldn't see her face very well because of the reflection on the windows, but now I know why she was so familiar to me. It was Violet, and now…now she's here.

Storm stands and shines the light onto Ivy's wounded leg. "I'll ask you again. Is Paisley here somewhere?"

Ivy groans and her head falls to the side.

"Didn't you fucking hear me?" Storm growls.

Ivy says nothing. Then, Storm places her foot on Ivy's ankle and pushes down hard. I cover my ears as Ivy's agonizing screams rush through the forest. Tears run from my eyes and sting the small scrapes on my face.

The two women laugh, then Storm tells Violet to go and get Thorn and Wolf so they can carry Ivy back to the house. As soon as Violet disappears into the trees, I creep closer to Storm and Ivy. I see a stout piece of branch on the ground and pick it up.

Storm sits next to Ivy. Both are silent as Storm randomly shines the flashlight into the trees. Then, she starts to sing. "*I guess you'd say, what can make me feel this way? My girl.*"

Her voice evokes a rage deep inside me. *You sick bitch. I hate you with every grain of my being.*

"Where are you, my girl? I know you're out there, hiding. What do you think of your Ivy now?" She laughs, shining the light onto Ivy's dirt covered face. "It looks to me that you chose the wrong girl." She shines the flashlight back to the trees and slowly scans the perimeter. A couple of times, the light shines only inches from where I'm standing. I know I have little time before Violet and the goons get here. Whatever I'm going to do, I have to do it now.

My pulse quickens as I crouch down and creep around to the other side of the large rock. Every so often, the beam of light comes toward me and I hide behind a tree. Ivy moans, drowning out the sounds of my feet as I step closer to the rock. The back of Storm's head comes into view as I tightly grasp the thick branch in my hand.

"Where are you, Paisley? I know you're out there somewhere, I can feel you."

My heart is pounding so hard, it echoes in my ears. As I hold the stick high above my head, my legs start to shake and weaken, and I pray that they don't give out. Storm could have a gun or a knife on her, I wouldn't put it past her.

My feet are just about touching the bottom of the huge stone when Storm calls out, "Paisley, this is your last chance. If you don't come out right now, I'm going to make sure that your little bimbo never walks on her leg again."

Fueled by rage, I slam the stout piece of wood down hard on her head. Immediately I jump backward and drop the stick as she collapses to the ground. I stare at her motionless form, terrified and in shock. I can't believe I had the guts to actually do it.

I force a deep breath into my lungs and bend over. The sound of the wood hitting Storm's head echoes in my mind.

Then, I hear movement in front of me. Slowly, I raise my eyes to see Storm clambering to her feet—blood has trickled from a wound on head and is now trailing down one side of her face. She stares at me, her eyes furious and wild. "There you are. You've come to save your little Barbie Doll, have you?"

When she reaches into her pants pocket, I quickly grab the branch and hold it in front of me.

Storm laughs. "Have you decided to fight me face-to-face instead of sneaking up behind me like a chicken shit?"

I don't answer, I just steady my feet and keep my eyes locked on her. Storm takes a fast step toward me and more blood trickles down her face. She's just about to take another step when her eyes freeze, and she stops. She opens her mouth, but as soon as the first sound leaves her lips, her eyes close and she falls to the ground.

Knowing that we're losing time, I run over to the flashlight and pick it up. Holding it in between my teeth, I grab Storm by the arms and drag her as far as I can into the brush. I stand over her and point the light on her face. Her raven hair is matted with blood and stuck to her cheeks. Her eyes are closed. I've never caused injury to another human being before, but I feel nothing but hatred for her, and I find myself hoping she never gets up.

In a parody of what I did for Ivy, I cover her with leaves and twigs, hoping that she won't be found by Violet and the two thugs. When I'm finished, I quickly walk back to Ivy. Her head is still slumped over and she's moaning. I stroke her hair gently and tell her that everything is going to be ok.

"It's bad," she says, referring to her foot.

"I know, sweetie. But we're going to get it all fixed up."

"When Storm kept on stomping on it, I felt the bone go through the skin."

Even though I have the flashlight now, I can't look at her injury. It would weaken me, and I need all my strength to get us out of here. Gently, I pull her good foot to me and unlace the shoe, taking it off and slipping it onto my own filthy and cut-up foot.

"You won't make it with me, Paisley," Ivy mumbles. "Run as fast as you can away from here. Let the others have me. I'll only slow you down."

With a sudden boost of adrenaline, I hand Ivy the flashlight, then lift her onto my back once more.

As fast as I can, I carry her through the forest in the direction of the stream. For some reason, her weight isn't bothering me this time, nor are the sticks and twigs that scrape and cut at my bare skin. Before I know it, we're standing beside the stream.

I set Ivy down and cup water in my hands so she can drink. The cool water seems to make her more alert. She grins and uses her shirt to wipe some of the caked-on dirt from her face.

As we rest, my mind reflects on everything we've been through. It's obvious now that Storm and Violet set this whole thing up, a sinister plan to get Ivy and me to come up with fifty grand. A wave of anger rises in me as I imagine Storm and Wolf parked somewhere nearby while Ivy was stuffed in the dark cellar. I feel so stupid for believing that Storm was the victim and Wolf was the murderer.

Now that we can follow the stream to the road, I have to get rid of the light. It's like a beacon, signaling to the others where we are. I tell Ivy to wait while I walk to the top of the small embankment on the other side of the water. There, I throw the light as far as I can down the stream. With luck, it may distract Violet and the goons, giving Ivy and I more time to get away.

* * *

With Ivy on my back again, we follow the stream. But after about fifteen minutes, Ivy's body suddenly goes rigid and she tells me to stop.

"What's wrong? Is it the pain?"

"No. Can't you hear them?"

I set Ivy down and listen. I hear nothing and for a moment it occurs to me that she may be hallucinating from the pain. I'm just about to convince her that we should resume walking when off in the distance behind us, I hear faint voices.

"Let's move, Ivy. Now!"

She wraps her arms around my neck, and I quickly lift her. Knowing that they are probably gaining on us, I take longer and faster strides. But no matter how much faster I'm trudging, the voices get louder, closer. After about ten minutes, I can make out Thorn's voice as he hollers, "Hey, look at the light down the stream. We're going the wrong way."

Then I hear Violet's voice. It rakes through my brain like nails on a chalkboard. "Storm? Storm, are you there?"

"It's working, Ivy," I whisper happily. "They're going to walk down to the light."

"You're so clever, Paisley," she says weakly.

"Desperate, not clever!"

We walk a few more minutes before I stop for a short rest, setting Ivy down on a tree stump. I gather more water from the stream for

231

us and then sit beside her. She wraps her arm around my waist and puts her head on my shoulder. Over the last while, I've noticed her breathing has become more labored and strained. I need to get her medical attention.

We agree that we should keep on moving and just as I stand, Violet yells from downstream, "You stupid ass, Thorn. It was a diversion. They must have done something to Storm and then taken off. Both of you go back to the property and get the car. There's a road somewhere around here and we need to get there before they do."

"Oh no. Paisley, they're going to find us and kill us. I know it." Ivy's breathing becomes more strained as she gasps for air.

Even though I can feel myself start to panic as well, I have to keep her calm, otherwise she'll run out of air and pass out, making it impossible to pack her.

"Ivy, stop it. You've got to stay focused and slow your breathing. I need you."

Her breathing shakes as she tries her hardest to exhale slowly to calm herself down.

I heft her onto my back and walk hard and fast alongside the water. With every step I take, a shiver runs up my back. I want to turn around to see if Violet is behind us, but I know that if I do, my fear will get the best of me and slow me down. Every second is vital right now.

We come to an incline and then I notice the rusty tunnel. As we walk uphill, the stream stays level.

"Ivy, we did it. We've reached the tunnel that goes under the road."

"We have?" she says, letting out a weak sob.

"Yes. Only a tiny bit more and we're there."

And for the first time, there's hope.

After some complicated movements, requiring me to put Ivy down and move broken branches, then pick her up again, we take the final step out of the dark maze of the forest and onto the flat gravel road. Above us, the sky is open and littered with bright stars. A feeling of elation warms me, regardless how physically and mentally exhausted I am.

I lower Ivy onto her strong foot, and she wraps her arms around my neck. She smiles. "Thank you for coming back for me."

I kiss her softly on the lips. The smell of musky dirt emanates from her.

It's probably getting close to sun-up and there are always people coming and going in the wee hours around here. The local farmers rise early to feed and milk their cows, and the Merville store owners live only a few miles from here. They take this route early every day.

"What about Thorn and Wolf?" Ivy asks. "Violet told them to get their car and find the road."

"I know. But they have a long way to go to get back to the house. Then, they have to drive all the way around the property to get here. We still have time."

Even though I say the words, I know I'm just as worried as she is. The truth is, if those two thugs ran or even walked back to their car, it wouldn't take them long to find us. My stomach clenches as I hold Ivy against me. What if we don't get out of this? What if Thorn and Wolf reach us before help arrives? Shielding my face from hers, involuntary tears roll down my cheeks. We were so close, but we could die just as easily here, inches from the finish line.

"Paisley, look!"

I turn and look behind me. Two small lights linger at the end of the road. Ivy laughs, tears streaking down her face. It is too soon for them to have gotten the car. It has to be.

*Please don't let it be them. We tried so hard to make it. After everything we've gone through, it can't end like this.*

"They're getting closer," she says.

I close my eyes and breathe deeply while the feeling of impending doom chokes me.

Ivy starts waving her hands as the lights near. She lunges toward the road, temporarily forgetting about her injured leg. I pull her back as the car approaches. As soon as the vehicle rolls up to us, my eyes focus on the driver. He's young, about thirty, and neither Thorn nor Wolf. I feel weak with relief.

He winds down the window of the dusty blue car and leans over. "You gals lost?" He has a friendly face and is wearing a baseball cap and a t-shirt.

Ivy bursts into tears. "Please, can you help us?"

As the man asks Ivy what happened, I see a quick flicker of light in my peripheral view. It's coming from the forest, the exact same place where Ivy and I just walked out of.

"Hey, let's continue this conversation in the car, ok?" I urge.

He nods and I open the back door, ushering Ivy in first. I slide in beside her and just as I'm pulling the door closed, I see Violet appear from the dark woods beside the road. She's only feet away.

"Hey, who's that? Did you girls lose a friend?" he says, looking past us through the back window.

"No!" we scream in unison. "Drive!"

"What's going on here?" says the driver, watching as Violet quickly approaches.

She tries the backdoor, but it's locked. She's just about to grab the front passenger's door handle when I see the flash of silver from the gun.

"She has a gun!" I yell. "Drive!"

Apparently he sees it too, because he steps on the gas so hard that Ivy and I are thrust backward.

As we speed away, I watch Violet aim the weapon. When it goes off, the car swerves as the driver starts to panic. "What the hell?"

"They were trying to kill us," shrieks Ivy.

"Why didn't you call the cops?" he demands.

"They took our phones," I answer.

"Who's that?" the driver says, looking in his rear-view mirror.

Ivy and I quickly turn around and look out of the back window. Headlights shine from behind us. There's no doubt in my mind who it is—Wolf and Thorn. I watch as the car stops briefly and a door opens, and Violet jumps in. They speed to catch up, closing the gap between us.

"We're going to die, aren't we?" Ivy asks, choking up.

"Not today," the driver says, stepping on the accelerator.

Despite this, the car behind us gains ground and before we know it, they're ramming into our bumper, causing the car to fish-tail on the loose gravel. The driver curses as he clenches the wheel and focuses on the road ahead. "Screw this," he says. "Hang on, girls. I've got an idea. The back of my father's property is just up ahead."

I put my arms around Ivy and squeeze her into me. As the thugs and Violet tail us, our driver watches the sides of the road intently. Just as the car behind rams us again, he suddenly cranks the wheel. We slide sideways as the car turns off the gravel and down a barely visible side road, no bigger than a lane.

"What the hell are you doing?" I yell, trying to hold onto Ivy.

"Trust me, nobody knows this property like I do," the guy says. In the mirror, I can see his jaw set with determination.

I look behind us and see the front end of the sedan bounce as they follow us down the rough terrain.

"Is this even a road?" I ask.

"It's more of a dead end," he says.

"What? Why the hell did you turn down here?"

He steps on the gas and speeds up, the car creaking as we jump up and down over the uneven ground. I continue watching the car behind us as they gain speed.

"Ok. Hang on," he says, before grabbing the wheel and cranking it. The car sharply careens left, crashing through the thicket. The thugs behind us don't turn in time. Instead, they continue straight. Our car comes to a sudden stop as dust and debris shoot up from the sedan's back tires, creating a huge dirt cloud. A moment later we hear a huge bang and the crunch of crumpling metal.

The driver tells us to stay in the car while he goes to check on the wreckage. Ivy and I beg him not to go. He doesn't listen. I lean forward and ready myself. I'll jump over the seat and behind the wheel if I hear a gunshot.

Ivy and I stare out the back window and watch as white smoke billows from the sedan. The doors are closed, and the hood is crumpled and sticking up above the front of the car. Slowly, our driver approaches the sedan. My heart races and it's hard to swallow. I picture Violet kicking open the back door and opening fire on the driver. I can hear Ivy hyperventilate beside me.

The driver bends down and looks in the windows, then slowly backs away. Next, we see him grab his stomach and vomit onto the dirt. After a moment or two, he wipes his mouth on the back of his hand then walks back to the car.

As soon as he slides in behind the wheel, we ask him what he saw.

"Never mind. I don't want to talk about it."

"Well, will you at least tell us if anyone is still alive?"

"I couldn't tell. All I know is that one of the passengers lost most of his head."

# Chapter Fourteen

Over the next couple of days, I'm inundated with doctors, counselors and detectives. The doctors put me on a mild tranquilizer to help me relax. I guess the reason for the therapists is because I've been screaming in my sleep.

I've only been able to see Ivy twice since we got here. The doctor tells me that she had to have surgery on her foot where they put steel plates over the bone. When she was in post-op, I was wheeled to her room. She was out cold, but I sat with her and held her hand for as long as they'd let me.

I tried to sneak down to see her the morning after, but because of the drugs they have me on, I was dizzy and fell as soon as I entered the hall.

The local paper showcased a really great picture of Jasper from many years ago when he was in the military. I've kept it under my pillow so I can take it out and look at it. Even though he didn't succeed at getting away, he risked his life for Ivy and me. I owe him a huge debt. I'll never forget the night he came over and how much fun the three of us had watching TV and drinking wine. I hope that wherever he is has endless wine and movies. And Madonna.

The paper also mentioned that the driver that rescued us is a real hero. Apparently, his name is Billy. He works for his father on a farm near to where he picked Ivy and me up. I can't wait to get out of here so I can call him up and thank him for saving our lives.

Wolf died from massive head injuries. Violet and Thorn survived and are being treated in the hospital, cuffed to their beds and with cops in their rooms. As for Storm—she lived. From what the detective said, she was knocked unconscious when I hit her, but only experienced a mild concussion. She's being held in Courtenay pre-trial, awaiting the rest of the charges. Ivy needs to be more alert before the detective can properly interview her. However, the detective did reassure me that Storm, Violet and Thorn won't get out for a long time, if they ever get out at all.

I've been spending a lot of time chatting on the phone, not with my mom, but with my father. Apparently when he heard what happened, he broke down. My mother said that he was overcome with worry and guilt over the way he's been treating me. It's funny how when we come close to losing someone we love, all of the bullshit falls away. Dad explained that his bad attitude toward me has been predicated on worry, not resentment. He also said that he has no problem with me being gay, he only ever had issues about how people would judge me for it.

Dad said as soon as I'm better, he's stealing me away for a fishing trip. I can't wait.

Ivy told her parents about falling in love with me. Apparently, they weren't surprised at all. And right after they found out, my mother called me, all happy and excited. She said that she knew all along that Ivy and I were attracted to each other, even if we didn't. She claims to have known because of how much energy we spent hating one another.

* * *

"Hey, are you going to just stand there or help me with these boxes?"

I rush over to Ivy and lift one of the items from her arms. After six months of staying in a rental cabin, we finally have our own place—on Texada, of course. Both my parents and Ivy's got together the down payment for a pretty little bungalow by the sea. Dad and I went to Nanaimo to pick out furniture together.

Ivy and I walk into the living room, set down the boxes and look out over the bay. "Are you glad we're here?" she asks, slipping her hand into mine. She lifts her foot from the ground to give it a rest—even after all these months, it still gives her some pain. It should fade with time.

"I'm glad I'm anywhere with you," I tell her. "Even when you piss me off."

She smiles then kisses me.

"Hey, this is from our parents," she says, pulling something from her pocket. She passes me an envelope.

It's addressed to both of us. Ivy watches as I carefully open the letter before reading it aloud. " 'To our brave girls. We hope you're happy in your new place. Please try not to burn it down because we can't afford to help you get another one. With love, The Parents.' "

There are a couple of tickets in the envelope. I read the front of one and then laugh as I pass them to Ivy.

*Couples Cooking Classes: For Beginners*

The End

If you enjoyed this book, please leave the author a review.

*Jay Lang books published by BWL Publishing Inc.*

*Hush*

*Shatter*

*Shiver*

*Storm*

Jay Lang grew up on the ocean, splitting her time between Read Island and Vancouver Island before moving to Vancouver to work as a TV, film and commercial actress. Eventually she left the industry for a quieter life on a live-a-board boat, where she worked as a clothing designer for rock bands. Five years later she moved to Abbotsford to attend university. There, she fell in love with creative writing and wrote five novel manuscripts in a year. She spends her days hiking and drawing inspiration for her writing from nature.

BWL Publishing

bwlpublishing.ca